A Shrine of Murders

"There comes at nightfall to that hostelry
Some nine and twenty in a company,
Of divers persons who had happened to fall
In comradeship and pilgrims they were all
Who towards Canterbury town they would ride."
(Chaucer's *Canterbury Tales,* "The Prologue")

"In the Middle Ages women doctors continued to practise in the midst of wars and epidemics as they always had, for the simple reason that they were needed."
Kate Campbellton Hurd-Mead. *A History of Women in Medicine.* London: The Haddam Press, 1938. Page 306.

A Shrine of Murders

Being the First of the Canterbury Tales of Kathryn Swinbrooke, Leech and Physician

C. L. Grace

St. Martin's Press
New York

Editor: George Witte
Production Editor: Mara Lurie
Copyeditor: Erica Schmid
Designer: Basha Zapatka

Library of Congress Cataloging-in-Publication Data

Grace, C. L.
A shrine of murders / C.L. Grace.
p. cm.
ISBN 0-312-09388-8
1. Women detectives—England—Canterbury—Fiction. 2. Great Britain—History—Lancaster and York, 1399–1485—Fiction. I. Title.
PR6054.O37S55 1993
823'.914—dc20 93-474
CIP

First Edition: May 1993

10 9 8 7 6 5 4 3 2 1

This novel is dedicated to the memory of the late Dr. William Urry, scholar and ardent student of medieval Canterbury. I must also express my gratitude to Dr. Urry's daughter, Mrs. Elizabeth Wheatley, who kindly allowed me access to her late father's papers on medieval Canterbury. Any errors, however, rest solely with me, and certainly not with that great scholar.

Author's Note

History is riddled with as many fallacies as facts. It is easy to assume that, in the Middle Ages, the status of women was negligible and only succeeding centuries saw a gradual improvement in their general lot. This is certainly incorrect. One famous English historian has already pointed out that women probably had more rights in 1300 than they had in 1900, whilst Chaucer's description of the Wife of Bath shows a woman who could not only hold her own in a world of men but travelled all over Europe to the great shrines and was a shrewd business woman, ever-ready to hold forth on the superiority of the gentler sex.

In this novel fiction corresponds with fact and the quotation facing the title page summarises quite succinctly how women played a vital role as doctors, healers and apothecaries. Kathryn Swinbrooke may be fiction, but in 1322, the most famous doctor in London was Mathilda of Westminster; Cecily of Oxford was the royal physician to Edward III and his wife Philippa of Hainault; and Gerard of Cremona's work (mentioned in the novel) clearly describes women doctors during the medieval period. In England, particularly, where the medical faculties at the two universities Oxford and Cambridge were relatively weak, women did serve as doctors and apothecaries, professions only in later centuries denied to them.

History does not move in a straight line but often in circles, and this certainly applies to medieval medicine. True, as today, there were charlatans ready to make a 'quick shilling' with so-called miraculous cures, but medieval doctors did possess considerable skill, particularly in their powers of observation and diagnosis. Some of their remedies, once dismissed as fanciful, are today in both Europe and America regarded quite rightly as alternative medicine.

Historical Personages Mentioned in the Text

In 1471 the Wars of the Roses between the Houses of Lancaster and York reached their climax in the two battles of Barnet and Tewkesbury, which led to the total destruction of Lancaster and the ascendancy of the House of York.

Edward IV, Yorkist King 1461–1470; 1471–1483.
Elizabeth Woodville, Edward IV's wife.
George, Duke of Clarence, brother to Edward IV.
Richard, Duke of Gloucester, younger brother to Edward IV.

Henry VI, Lancastrian King, murdered in the Tower 1471.
Margaret of Anjou, the "She-Wolf," Henry VI's wife and the main protagonist of the House of Lancaster.
Beaufort, Duke of Somerset, Margaret of Anjou's principal general (and, if scandal is to be believed, the Queen's lover).
Lord Wenlock, Lancastrian general.
Richard Neville, Earl of Warwick, Lancastrian general nicknamed the "Kingmaker."
Thomas Falconberg, Lancastrian general. He made the last stand trying to hold London after the Yorkish victory at Tewkesbury.
Edward, son of Margaret of Anjou, killed at Tewkesbury.

Henry IV, King of England, 1399–1413.
John Wycliffe, English ecclesiastical reformer in the last quarter of the fourteenth century.
Nicholas Faunte, Mayor of Canterbury and ardent Lancastrian.
Thomas à Becket, Archbishop of Canterbury. He clashed with Henry II (1154–1189) over the rights of the church

and was murdered in Canterbury by a party of Henry's knights.

Geoffrey Chaucer (c.1340–1400), poet, diplomat and courtier. England's greatest medieval poet and author of the *Canterbury Tales.*

Main Streets of Canterbury, c.1471

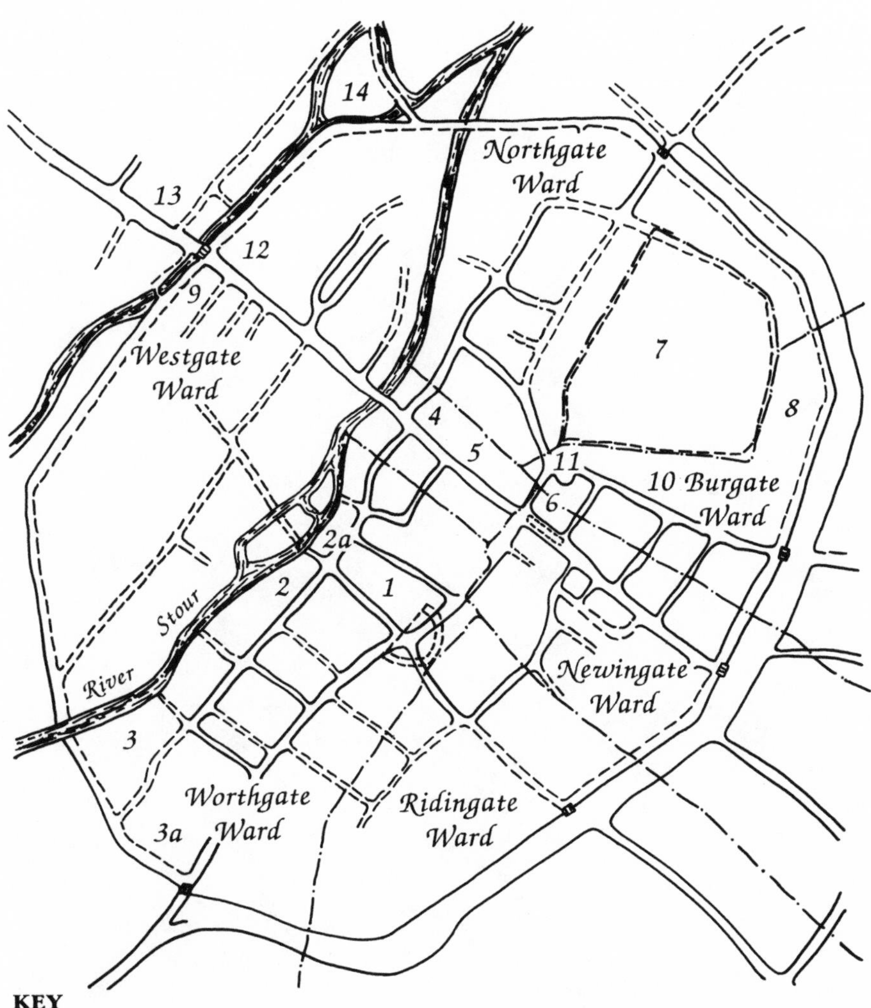

KEY

1 = **Ottemelle Lane**
2 = **Hethenman Lane**
2a = **Poor Priests' Hospital**
3 = **St. Mildred's Church**
3a = **Canterbury Castle**
4 = **High Street**
5 = **Guildhall**
6 = **The Mercery**
7 = **Christchurch Cathedral Buildings**
8 = **Queningate**
9 = **Holy Cross Church**
10 = **Burgate**
11 = **Buttermarket/Bullstake**
12 = **Westgate**
13 = **Fastolf Inn**
14 = **Kingsmead**

Prologue

Wizards and warlocks proclaimed it to be a killing time. Squatting in their damp cells, the monkish scribes dipped quills in ink-horns and wrote a chronicle of their years, neatly cataloguing the homicides, felonies, treasons and bloody deaths. The good monks really believed the Gates of Hell were prevailing. After all, so the gossips said, on the Eve of All Hallows past, the necromancer John Marshall took seven pounds of wax and two ells of cloth to a deserted manor-house outside Maidstone and fashioned there rude puppets depicting the King, his Queen, and all the great nobles of the land. Marshall had dipped these in blood, pricked them with bodkins and left them to roast over a roaring fire. Deep in Bean Woods outside Canterbury, other magicians clad themselves in long skins, the hides of animals with immense tails still attached; they smutted their faces and called upon the witch-queen Herodias to come to their aid. Other sorcerers, so the chroniclers wrote, made bloody sacrifices to the Queen of the Night and called upon the ghouls for assistance. Strange sights were seen: legions of hags flew through the dark watches of the night, leading silent convoys of the dead to black sabbaths and blasphemous Masses.

Such whispering spread even to the city of Canterbury itself. A man with the head of a corpse and a grimoire of spells was arrested near Westgate, and outside the city limits, a woman who had murdered her husband had a rod struck through her mouth, a spike through her head; yet when she was buried, her flesh still quivered. Other evils swept in as spring gave way to summer. The demon sweating sickness appeared, its victims dying in a few hours: some in sleep, some whilst walking, some fasting, others full of food. The sickness always began with a pain in the head, then the heart; nothing could cure it. All remedies were tried: the horn of a unicorn, dragon's water, angelica root. Prayers were offered, relics brought, heaven beseeched, but Death still strode the foul alleyways and streets of Canterbury. His skull-like face grinned through the windows, his bony fingers tapped on doors or rattled on casements in his voracious hunt for victims.

Summer came at last. The sweating sickness disappeared but the violence and blood-lust continued. Strange deaths were reported, mysterious fatalities amongst those who flocked to Canterbury to seek the help of Blessed Thomas à Becket, whose battered corpse and cloven skull lay under sheets of gold before the high altar of Canterbury Cathedral. Of course, the living ignored the dead, and at first the murders went unnoticed. After all, summer was here. The streets were dry, the grass was long and lush, the water sweet and fresh. A time for travelling, for visiting friends. Folk gathered in their orchards, sipping cool wine or draining tankards of the ale they'd brewed during the winter months. They discussed the blood-drenched prophecies, the failings of their betters, and above all the bitter civil war raging between the houses of York and Lancaster.

In the west the Wolf Queen, Margaret of Anjou, plotted with her generals to seize the throne for her witless husband, King Henry VI, and their son, her golden boy Edward. Her enemies mocked her and said her husband was so holy, he had not the wit nor the means to beget an heir and that the young prince was the offspring of her secret lust for Beaufort, Duke of Somerset. In London, Edward of York, with his silver-haired wife, Elizabeth Woodville, and his war-hungry brothers Clarence and Gloucester, gathered in the King's secret chamber at Westminster and drew up subtle plans against the She-Wolf's approach. They attended Mass three times a day, sang Matins and Vespers, and all the time plotted the total destruction of Margaret, her husband, and the entire House of Lancaster. Truly a killing time, and those who could remembered the sombre lines of Chaucer's poem about

> *"The smiling rascal, concealing knife in cloak;*
> *The farm barns burning and the thick black smoke.*
> *The treachery of murder done in bed,*
> *The open battle and the wounds which bled."*

A few weeks later Robert Clerkenwell, a physician from Aldgate in London, was busy conversing about the fortunes of such a war in the Checker Board Tavern near the stocks in the centre of Canterbury. Robert was a rich man; the physic he'd sold during the sweating sickness, rosewater and honey, may not have cured many of his patients, but it had earned the good doctor clinking purses of gold and silver. Robert thought he'd had a good year.

'The Lord giveth and the Lord taketh away,' he would murmur piously as he collected his fees and left his patients to die.

Now that summer had come, Robert had decided to thank God for such favours with a pleasant ride to Canterbury to pray before Becket's tomb. The journey had been peaceful, the countryside quiet and sweet, as if the land held its breath whilst kings and princes manoeuvred to fight. Clerkenwell had been in Canterbury three days;

he'd visited the cathedral twice, eaten good meals in the cook-shops and taverns of the city and even paid for the service of a comely wench who, upstairs in the tavern's most spacious chamber, had obliged him in every way he wished. Tomorrow he would leave; his bags were packed and the good doctor had just eaten his last meal at Canterbury or anywhere else: roast quail, golden, succulent and tender to the taste-buds; fresh vegetables, and clear white wine cooled in the tavern's spacious cellars. Now Robert sat back, burping gently, and beamed at his companions seated on either side of him in the great taproom.

'You mark my words,' he said, squeezing his pert lips together and patting his expansive stomach. 'Queen Margaret will be victorious: she has sturdy Bretons in her retinue, and Somerset and Wenlock are capable generals. Edward of York will be hard-pressed to keep what he has grasped.'

Clerkenwell's blue watery eyes glared round, but the other pilgrims were too tired or too drunk to care. Moreover, their companion the doctor was a tight-fisted man. They'd all hoped that before the evening was ended, he would ask the landlord to broach a new barrel of wine or at least order plates of roast meat or dishes of comfits to share among his still hungry and less fortunate companions. The physician smacked his lips and looked around. He picked up his goblet, ponderously swirled the lees and drained them in one gulp. He sat forward and glared.

'I want more wine! Hell's bones! Where is that boy?'

A servitor, his apron stained with particles of food and slops of wine, hurried up, his greasy, uncombed hair masking his face.

'You're not the fellow who served me last time!' the doctor bellowed. 'Hell's teeth, I want more wine!'

The servant nodded, took the cup and hurried away. A few minutes later he returned, the goblet brimming and bubbling, and sat it down carefully before the doctor. The other pilgrims glanced at each other and some began to stir restlessly. Obviously the physician was not to be their benefactor. Robert sipped the white wine, relishing its coolness on his tongue and the back of his mouth. He drank again, licking his lips, unaware of the deadly poison now seeping into his stomach, aiming like an arrow for his heart and brain. The doctor stirred; he felt uncomfortable, his belly churned, his heart began to flutter, his breath came in short gasps. He stood up, scrabbling at his collar, his whole body now in pain, as if licked by some invisible flame. The other pilgrims stared in open-mouthed horror as this loquacious physician, eyes popping out, face bright red, gasped, choked and fought for his life before falling dead on the spot.

As Clerkenwell died in Canterbury, so did his prophecies about the war at Tewkesbury in the West Country. The struggle had lasted all day, leaving Edward of York the victor. The Lancastrians had been broken, and the red-coated soldiers of Queen Margaret and the Duke of Somerset were fleeing from the blood-soaked battlefield. They surged up past Tewkesbury Abbey, across the meadows, desperately seeking a ford or bridge across the river Severn. Behind them the Yorkists howled like wolves and streamed in pursuit beneath the flapping blue banners bearing the Gold Sun of York or the Red Boar Rampant of the King's brother Richard, Duke of Gloucester. Cursing and growling, the Lancastrians pressed into the river. Drowned bodies began to choke the shallows, and the living trod upon them in their hope of escape. All around them swept their killers, screaming and shouting, thrusting with spear or hewing with sword, mace and club, sparing no one until the river shallows and the reeds growing there turned crimson-scarlet with bright gushing blood.

Colum Murtagh stood on the brow of a hill and watched the massacre. He turned his rowan-berry horse, took off his helmet and threw it down, cursing at the sweat which soaked his dark hair and blurred his vision.

He kept well away from the fighting. He was lightly armed with leather jerkin, sword and dagger and, Deo gratias, it was not his task to kill. The King had insisted on this. He and the other royal messengers were to stay clear, to carry orders between the different battles and, if the enemy broke, to spy out where their leaders would flee. Murtagh stared at the river glinting in the sunlight and gently patted his horse's neck.

'The poor die there,' he muttered, 'the poor, sodding commoners!' He studied the melee, trying to seek out banners, colours and liveries of great Lancastrian lords, but he could glimpse none. He turned and stared back towards the great abbey. 'Where was Somerset and the rest?' He strained his green, cat-like eyes, trying to distinguish between the different movements along the winding country lanes. Murtagh shifted his gaze as a flash of colour caught his attention. Yes, he saw them: a small party of horsemen carrying no banners, wearing no livery, with helmets and armour tossed aside, were riding across the abbey grounds away from the battle. Any other spy would have dismissed them as a group of common knights seeking refuge in flight, but Murtagh knew horses, and these were the best. He turned his own mount and spurred it quickly down the hill to a group of Yorkist commanders who stood clustered at a small crossroads round their golden-haired King. They turned at the rider dashing wildly towards them. Murtagh jumped off his horse, and falling to one knee before the King, pointed to beyond the hedgerows.

'Your Majesty,' he gasped, 'the Lancastrian commanders and their henchmen are fleeing west, away from the river.'

Under his crowned helmet, Edward of York's hard face broke into a grin. He flicked his fingers and issued a series of curt orders to a knight banneret of his household before turning to pat Murtagh on the shoulder.

'You've done well, Irishman,' he murmured. 'The reward is yours.'

By late afternoon the killing at the river had stopped. The Lancastrian commanders, seeing their escape route cut off by Yorkist forces, had turned, seeking sanctuary in the dark cool nave of Tewkesbury Abbey. But, as the chroniclers wrote, this was a killing time and the Yorkist soldiers followed them in. The serene silence of the abbey was broken by the clash of swords, the shouts of fighters and the groans and shrieks of wounded and dying men. The Lancastrians at last reached the sanctuary and, grasping the corners of the altar, claimed the protection of the Church. The Abbot himself appeared, carrying the golden cross of his office, thundering out excommunication at any who spilled blood on sacred ground.

The Yorkist soldiers sullenly withdrew, but King Edward gave the Abbot a warning: either the prisoners were handed over, or the abbey would be besieged. At last the Lancastrian commanders emerged, haggard, dishevelled, a mass of wounds from head to toe. They did not beg for the pardon they knew would not be theirs. The King's own brother, the wire-haired, slightly hunchbacked Richard of Gloucester, was appointed their judge. He set up a summary court just outside the abbey gates. One by one the King's enemies were taken before him for summary condemnation, and as the evening sun set, the Lancastrian commanders were hustled to the block on a makeshift scaffold in Tewkesbury market-place and their heads lopped off.

Colum Murtagh watched the first execution from a tavern window and turned away in disgust. He had played his part. There was further work to do, but it would be well away from the carnage of the killing ground. He put his hand into his wallet and felt the two warrants neatly folded there. The first made him custodian of the King's horses in the meadows outside Canterbury. The second gave him powers to investigate and report on the dreadful poisonings being carried out in the city. Murtagh lay back on the cot-bed, trying to close his ears to the thud of the executioner's axe. He would go to Canterbury; he'd be free of war, and safe, perhaps, from the Hounds of Ulster and their constant plots against him.

Chapter 1

'What you need is a man.'

'I have a man. I am married.' Kathryn Swinbrooke glared at Thomasina's fat white face.

The latter wiped the sweat from her brow and mopped her plump cheeks with a cloth. She put down the gutting-knife amongst the giblets of the chicken she had been cutting and smiled knowingly.

'I have known you since you were thumb-high to a buttercup, Mistress. Aye, you are married, but your husband's gone, fled to the wars, and the ugly bastard won't be back.' She sniffed.

'You need a man. A woman is not happy unless she has got a man between her thighs. I should know; I have been married three times."

Kathryn looked away and smiled. It was hard to imagine anyone between Thomasina's tree-trunk thighs.

'Did they wear chain-mail?' she muttered.

'What was that?'

'Nothing, Thomasina.'

Kathryn gathered her black hair, lightly streaked with grey, and edged it under her white linen veil, adjusting the red cord which kept it in place. She stared round the stone-flagged kitchen. Thomasina must have been up early, for already the place was scrubbed, the stone floor gleaming white, the table-top soft to the touch after the buckets of hot water poured across it. Even the hooded mantel above the fire glowed white, whilst the bronze skillet and fleshing-hooks hanging above the fire gleamed like burnished gold. Kathryn sighed, rose, slipping her feet into unlatched sandals. She lifted the hem of her green woollen dress, for the floor was still slightly damp after Thomasina's scrubbing.

'Satan's balls!' Thomasina muttered. She remembered the bread baking in the small oven beside the fire and waddled over with a wooden spatula, screaming for Agnes the young maid to come and help her.

Kathryn stopped at the half-open door and went to stand under the wooden porch, staring down at the garden. Once upon a time she had loved it—the sweet-smelling grass, the banks of wild-flowers and the carefully tended herb-plots, especially now, on a warm summer's day. In the white sunlight the garden lost some of its air of menace. She absent-mindedly dabbed at the nape of her neck. She felt warm in her underdress of woollen kirtle and green cord-bound gown.

'You look like a nun,' Thomasina grumbled. 'Whatever would your father say?'

'Father's dead,' Kathryn replied. 'Cold, buried under the slabs of Saint Mildred's Church.'

She blinked and stared down the garden. She still missed him. Dead six months, his soul gone to Purgatory and his dreadful secret bequeathed to Kathryn, his only child. She still could hardly believe it. She might learn to forget if those damned letters stopped coming. Kathryn felt inside her purse and drew out the yellow piece of parchment, pushed under the door the previous evening, thumb-marked, ragged and dirty. She studied the scrawled message: 'Where is Alexander Wyville? Where is your husband? Murder is a felony and felons hang!' Beside the words, a rude scaffold had been drawn. What chilled Kathryn's blood was the figure, roughly drawn with long hair and the gown of a woman, which dangled from the scaffold. 'Silence is golden,' the message continued. 'And the gold can be left upon Goodman's tomb in Saint Mildred's Churchyard.'

Kathryn screwed the paper up and put it back into her purse. She had received two similar messages since her father's death and desperately wondered who this sinister writer was and how he had learnt of her father's secret. So far she had paid no money, but the anonymous letter-writer was becoming more threatening, more insistent. She jumped as Thomasina came up behind her.

'We must go, Mistress.'

Kathryn became aware of the sounds around her, especially the bells of the cathedral booming under the lighter tone of other church bells. The alderman's writ had said noon. She stepped back into the kitchen and looked at where the hour-candle stood in its recess just near the buttery door. She screwed her eyes up and stared. Yes, the tenth circle had already been reached. Kathryn looked angrily at the flame eating away at her time, perhaps her freedom, perhaps even her life. She swallowed nervously. What did the alderman want? To ask her questions? The summons, sealed with the common seal of the city of Canterbury, had been quite curt. She was to present herself to the alderman in the Guildhall at twelve o'clock on Wednesday.

'What do they want?' she murmured to herself.

'God knows, Mistress,' Thomasina piped up behind her. 'But you know the council, an idle group of bastards. You'd think they'd have enough on their minds. I mean, the Mayor is an adjudged traitor. They say he is in hiding. The rest of the council must be wearing their brown leggings, for they supported the Lancastrians, and Edward the Golden Boy has dashed their hopes.'

Kathryn nodded and leaned against the door lintel.

Thomasina was right; she couldn't understand it. The great ones on the Canterbury Council had supported the Lancastrian cause: its mayor, Nicholas Faunte, had even led soldiers off to help Falconberg, the Lancastrian general holding London. Now all was lost. Edward of York had defeated the Lancastrians at Barnet before marching west to capture Margaret, their Queen, at Tewkesbury. The war was over. York had won and Lancaster and Canterbury had lost. Nicholas Faunte, its mayor, had been proclaimed a traitor with a price on his head, and the city was frightened it would lose its liberties. So why was the chief alderman busying himself with her? Surely they had enough on their plates with the end of the war.

Thomasina came round and faced her squarely, staring into the severe face of her mistress. The maid glowered to hide her surge of compassion. Kathryn was no beauty at the best of times; under her jet-black hair, her face could be too severe, the grey eyes hard, the olive skin invariably pale, the nose too aquiline; and those lips, which used to smile or make sardonic observations on the world, had been all too harsh since her father's death.

'Mistress,' Thomasina repeated, 'we must go!'

She handed Kathryn her dark blue cloak, her best, with its steep hood lined with miniver.

'We must call into the hospital, and you cannot be late. You might need the council's protection.'

Kathryn nodded absent-mindedly, put the cloak over the table and went down the passageway to her own chamber. She had to make sure everything was secure; the coffers containing the herbs and potions chained and padlocked. She could not afford to have someone breaking in and stealing a potion, only to die like Hawisa the pilgrim's wife who, to make herself more beautiful, had been stupid enough to drink a concoction distilled from laurel leaves and had died before anyone could do anything to help her. Kathryn stared round the chamber. Here, she most missed her father, amongst his horoscope charts, bowls, the tripod, cutting board, knife, needles and bottles of potions.

'You were a good physician,' she murmured, but the empty chamber mocked her with its silence. 'Everything is in order,' she snapped, as if angry with the room itself. Kathryn put the potions she'd prepared into a straw wicker basket and closed the door, turning the key and slipping it into her purse. She jumped as she heard a rap on the front door. Thomasina was at the far end of the scullery.

'I'll see to it,' Kathryn called.

She walked down the stone-flagged passageway, past the hall and the large open shop where her husband, Alexander, had once sold his spices, herbs and simples. She sighed at the dusty shelves, the cobwebs between the pots, jars and bottles, the counter an inch thick in dust. She would love to reorganise this, open the shop and continue her husband's trade. But she felt there was a bar, besides the lack of money, an iron chain across that path; for if she did, she would become her father's accomplice and be somehow responsible for his dreadful secret. The knocking on the door continued, chorused by childish yells.

'Mistress Swinbrooke! Mistress Swinbrooke!'

Peering through the squint-hole, Kathryn glimpsed the grimy faces of Edith and Eadwig, the twin children of Fulke the tanner, who lived in a tenement farther up Ottemelle Lane. Kathryn was tempted not to answer the knocking, but she took another glimpse at the children's pallid faces and slid the bolts back. The twins dashed in without invitation.

'Mistress Swinbrooke! Mistress Swinbrooke!'

Kathryn knelt and grabbed each by an arm, her heart lurching in compassion as she felt how thin the children were.

'What is the matter?' she asked.

'It's Father. He was treating some skins and he has burnt his arm.'

'Wait there!' Kathryn rose. 'No, on second thought, follow me.'

She went back into the kitchen, where Thomasina was pulling the bread-cage up into the rafters to keep the newly baked loaves away from foraging mice. Kathryn sat the children at the table.

'Keep your hands to yourselves!' Thomasina bellowed, glaring at the twins.

She tied the cord around the pulley to a hook on the wall and wiped her hands on the front of her apron. Then she came and stood over the children, winking secretly at Kathryn.

'I suppose you're hungry?' she shouted.

The two waifs looked at her, their mouths watering at the sweet smell of the new bread.

'There's nothing wrong with their father,' Thomasina muttered, turning to go into the larder to pour the children two tankards of buttermilk and a dish of marchpane. Kathryn left her to it and returned to her own chamber. She took down from the shelf her father's copy of Apuleius's *Herbarium* and the *Leech-Book* of Bald. She had to unlock the chains, for her father had always kept the precious books padlocked to the shelf. She knew the treatment for burns, but she always had to make sure. Kathryn satisfied herself before scooping two spoonfuls of paste into a piece of parchment and taking a thin roll of bandage from a small wicker hamper. She put everything back in its place, carefully screwed up the parchment with the paste in it and returned to the kitchen, where Edith and Eadwig were busy eating. She sat opposite them.

'Edith.'

The little girl looked up.

Kathryn pushed across the small package of ointment. 'Tell your father to keep the burn dry until a blister forms.

The bandage must be put on when the blister breaks. Once it has, cover it with paste and let the wound heal.'

'What's in it?' Edith piped up.

'Some crushed moss, a little wine, salt and vinegar.'

'How does it cure the burn?' Eadwig queried.

'We don't know,' Kathryn replied. 'All we know is that it will. If the wound is kept clean and allowed to dry, a nice scab appears.'

Edith pulled a face.

'Come on!' Thomasina urged. 'Children, you have to go!'

Kathryn went to wash her hands in the lead sink in the buttery whilst Thomasina shooed the children out and gave instructions to the young maid. Kathryn picked up her cloak and the brooch bought by her husband, wrought with rubies and sapphires to form the inscription: "I am here in the place of a friend I love." Kathryn fastened the robe absent-mindedly. Thomasina looked on; beneath her bluff exterior she was anxious about her mistress. Kathryn's husband had gone to the wars to disappear from the face of the earth. Had he run away? Thomasina wondered, or been killed and was buried in some mass grave? Alexander had been a personable young man, a good apothecary who had made an honest marriage with a doctor's daughter. He and Kathryn had only been married for seven months when he had left to serve with Faunte's troops in London.

So far Thomasina had kept her own counsel, but she had wondered if Alexander Wyville had been two people: the honest merchant and the drunken wife-beater. Thomasina had often heard her mistress's cries and sobs. On one occasion she had even glimpsed Alexander, wild-eyed, white-faced, lurching along the passageway. The old physician had also known, but he was too aged to intervene, so he could only grieve. Three months after Alexander had left, the old doctor had died. Thomasina had hoped things would improve, but her mistress seemed subdued, as if guarding a terrible secret.

By a fairy's tits! she thought. Why can't she just declare herself a widow and marry again? I've been married three times. Thomasina smiled to herself. If any of her husbands had laid a finger on her, she would have thumped them.

'Thomasina, why are you smiling?'

'Oh, its nothing, Mistress. Let's leave.'

Thomasina turned and shouted her orders at Agnes, then went down the passageway and out the front door into Ottemelle Lane. The day was proving to be a fine one and the sun was already baking the manure heaps; because of the disturbances in the city, the rakers had not been out and the sewers and cobbles were littered with festering garbage and reeking night-soil. At the corner of the lane, Rawnose the pedlar was standing with his tray slung around his neck by a tattered red ribbon. He called them over. Kathryn sighed and went across. She liked the old beggar ever since he had turned up asking her father's assistance to sew his ears, badly cropped, after he had been caught stealing for the third time. Nonetheless, Rawnose was still as garrulous as a jackdaw.

'You are well, Mistress? You have heard the news?'

Kathryn shook her head. Rawnose was better than any broadsheet.

'Two nights ago a physician was found dead at the Checker Board Tavern, poisoned he was. Nicholas Faunte the mayor is still in hiding. He has been proclaimed a traitor by the King, who has now reached London. Oh, have you heard the news of the witch outside Rochester?'

Kathryn just smiled.

'Died and had her body sewn in the hide of a stag. She was sheeted in a stone coffin, placed in the church and fifty psalms sung over it, but the Devil still came for her. He broke open the coffin with his cloven foot and plucked up the old witch's corpse, fastening it with hooks on his coal-black horse.'

'You shouldn't believe everything you hear,' Thomasina interrupted.

Rawnose stared at Thomasina and licked his lips, boldly admiring her ample breasts and broad hips.

'You'll come for a drink with me, Thomasina?'

'I'll dance with the Devil first!'

Thomasina linked her arm through Kathryn's and they went down an alley-way past the hovels of the poor. Kathryn could smell cabbage cooking, and through the open doors glimpsed the women in their homespun gowns carding and spinning wool. A few tiles in the centre of the earth-beaten floors served as a fireplace. A mass of rags in the corner was the communal bed, and the only ornament a rough-hewn crucifix. Children sat amongst dog turds chewing black bread rubbed with onion juice. Kathryn looked away and breathed a prayer. Sickness and plague would come, but she agreed with her father, a pupil of John Gaddesden, that such dirt, filth and poor food nourished epidemics, fevers and illnesses. They turned into Hethenman Lane, where the stalls were laid out on either side. The more powerful citizens strutted here: the men in their flounced jackets and tight multicoloured hose, their wives tucking up undershifts of silk away from the offal underfoot. Dressed in severe black taffeta and white veil, Widow Gumple flounced by them. Her nose and mouth wrinkled disdainfully at Kathryn, who smiled back.

'She looks as if she wants to fart,' Thomasina hissed, 'but cannot do it.'

Kathryn giggled. 'Have more charity, Thomasina.'

'She's a snotty-nosed bitch,' Thomasina answered her, 'who resents your work as a physician and because you won't join her coterie of hypocrites in the vestry-house at Saint Mildred's.' Thomasina stopped and glared at the Widow Gumple's retreating back.

'She is a hypocrite,' she repeated. 'I have heard the

stories of how she is sweet on a young student who gets well above her garters.'

'Shush! Shush!' Kathryn replied.

They walked on only to start at the red-haired figure which slipped from between the stalls. Kathryn quietly groaned and hoped the din of the market had drowned most of Thomasina's more colourful curses. Goldere the clerk stood there, his plump spoilt face twisted into a grimace which was supposed to be a smile, whilst his bony white fingers ruffled back lank red hair. His face always reminded Kathryn of a dissolute child, with its bleary eyes, squat nose and twisted lips. She often wondered if there was something wrong with his inner juices, for his attempts to grow a beard and moustache were pathetic—soft downy hairs which, Thomasina claimed, if covered with cream, a cat could lick off.

'Mistress Kathryn,' Goldere simpered. 'So pleased to see you. You are well?'

'We are in a hurry,' Thomasina spoke up.

'Good morrow, Master Goldere,' Kathryn added, stepping round him.

The clerk was not so easy to shake off but sidled up like a shadow. Kathryn tried not to wrinkle her nose at his sour smell.

'I wish to call on you, Mistress. I have certain ailments.'

'There are other healers, Master Goldere,' Kathryn replied. 'I am a leech and an apothecary, not your personal physician.'

'Then perhaps you can join me for a sup or a bite to eat?'

'Master Goldere, I am a married woman!'

'Ah, and how is your husband? Is there any news?'

Kathryn looked away. Was Goldere the sender of the messages? she wondered.

'There is gossip,' Goldere continued maliciously. 'Why do you not carry your husband's name?'

Kathryn stopped, her eyes blazing. Goldere stepped nervously back.

'Master Clerk,' Kathryn whispered hoarsely. 'You know the law. My husband, God assoil him, is probably dead. As his widow I can inherit, in my own name, his property. Now, sir, I bid you adieu!'

She swept on by, whilst Thomasina sidled up to Goldere.

'Master Clerk,' she whispered.

'Yes,' he rasped, frightened of this small but forbidding woman with her brown staring eyes in that white resolute face.

'Master Goldere. Are your bowels in good order?'

The clerk whirled round, his hand going to the hose stretched across his buttocks.

'I only wondered,' Thomasina added. She smiled beatifically and followed her mistress.

They went up Crimelende Street and into the Poor Priests' Hospital, a large two-storied stone building. Father Cuthbert the warden was waiting for them in his small oak-panelled chamber. He rose and warmly clasped Kathryn's hand.

'You are earlier than we expected, Mistress Swinbrooke.'

'I have other business to attend, Father.'

'Come, come!'

Father Cuthbert led her upstairs into a long hall of polished wood. Along each wall were carved bedsteads placed at right angles to the wall under long tracery windows filled with stained glass. Under the lofty timbered roof the walls were washed with lime, which enhanced an impression of space and coolness. Kathryn always marvelled at the cleanliness of the place. The straw-filled mattresses were suspended on cords fastened to four posts to allow the air to circulate and keep the room sweet; the sick, ageing priests lay on feather-filled bolsters between clean sheets covered by heavy grey counterpanes.

Kathryn undid the basket Thomasina carried and handed Father Cuthbert a small jar.

'This is saxifraga and parsley boiled in ale. It will ease Father Dunstan's bladder stone. And Benedict still suffers from dysentery?'

The priest nodded, smiling at Kathryn's business-like tones.

'He must be kept on good gruel,' Kathryn continued, 'and fed on this.' She handed over a second jar.

'What is it?'

'Honey and wheaten-meal boiled in salted fat with a little wax. It will help bind his stomach.'

'What about payment?' Father Cuthbert murmured.

'As is customary. At the end of every month Thomasina will bring you a bill." Kathryn smiled. 'I promise the cost won't be heavy. All is well here, Father?'

The priest shrugged and glanced fleetingly at the very demure Thomasina.

'Mistress Kathryn, death is inevitable. All we do is make the final meeting a little easier.' His sad old eyes studied Kathryn. 'You are well, Mistress Swinbrooke?'

Kathryn stared at this gentle priest. Cuthbert, in his grey sparse gown, with his humorous face and anxious eyes, always reminded Kathryn of a little mouse, full of the joys of spring but ever watchful. Should I tell him? Kathryn wondered. Would he shrive me of my sin? But how could she confess? How could she speak about a murder she couldn't prove and, despite the seal of confession, what would their relationship be afterwards? She bit her lips. And what about her father, whom this priest had loved? Father Cuthbert had gone to her father's deathbed and anointed his eyes, brow, mouth, hands and feet with holy oil. Cuthbert had shriven him and brought the sacrament for that last great journey. Kathryn blinked and looked away. Did the priest know?

Father Cuthbert also studied Kathryn. He felt the sadness in her and wished he could help. But how could he? He had bent his ear to hear her father's last gasping phrases. He had glimpsed the terror in the man's eyes and whispered back words of absolution, telling him to put his trust in God's infinite compassion. Every morning Father Cuthbert remembered physician Swinbrooke at Mass and wondered how he could share the dead man's secret with Mistress Kathryn. To do that he would have to break the seal of confession. The old priest had known Kathryn since she was a child, yet now they stood like strangers in this sun-washed hall. Even Thomasina, whom the priest had loved an eternity ago, seemed more distant and aloof.

'I must be going,' Kathryn muttered abruptly, so the priest ushered them out.

Chapter 2

As she and Thomasina left the hospital, Kathryn noticed her old nurse was quiet, as she invariably was when they met Father Cuthbert. Were the stories true? Kathryn wondered. She glanced sideways; Thomasina was as demure as a young lass, lost in some reverie. Had Thomasina been in love with the priest? Did she still love him?

Kathryn pressed Thomasina's hand. 'One day you should tell him,' she murmured.

'What, Mistress?'

'The truth!'

'I did once. I told him he was beautiful.' Thomasina cleared her throat and blinked furiously. 'He still is,' she whispered, but her words were lost in the din of the crowd as they entered the High Street, which ran under the brooding mass of Canterbury Cathedral. The crowd was more dense here; stalls stood on either side of a thoroughfare packed with carts, horses and, of course, troops of pilgrims. Some of these were solitary, others in organised groups. Some were clad in everyday dress; others wore flat-brimmed hats, grey cloaks and carried staves and scrips. Most were from surrounding towns and vil-

lages. A few were professional pilgrim-walkers and bore on their hats and cloaks the scallop-shell of St James Compostella or the engraved palm indicating they had even been to Jerusalem in Outremer. It was a fairly usual sight, people streaming up into the grounds of the cathedral to visit Becket's great shrine, but what caught Kathryn's attention were the anxious groups of burgesses clustered on the steps of the Guildhall.

'No need to ask what's worrying them,' Thomasina murmured.

Kathryn nodded. 'The aldermen of the Corporation,' she replied, 'are finding out what it's like to be on the losing side of a war.'

She pointed to the groups of soldiers, most of them covered in dust, their faces tired and lined with exhaustion. Edward of York's soldiers, fresh from victory in the West Country and eager to stamp their King's authority on this now disgraced city. The livery of York could be seen everywhere, soldiers wearing the White Rose or the Red Boar of Gloucester, the King's brother. Many of their citizens, eager to show their allegiance, had plucked white roses from their gardens and sported them in their beaver hats. A few of the leading burgesses' wives even wore them in their hair. As Kathryn and Thomasina climbed the Guildhall steps, they were roughly jostled by the King's soldiers streaming out, carrying chests full of documents, whilst a royal herald nailed a list of proscribed citizens, now judged traitors by the King, on the Guildhall door.

Kathryn and Thomasina entered the musty darkness of the Guildhall. They were immediately challenged by a royal serjeant who had an ugly bruise under his right eye and a suppurating cut on his left hand.

'What's your business?' he snapped.

A group of soldiers farther down the corridor heard the tone of his voice and approached to watch the sport.

'I am an apothecary, a physician,' Kathryn answered. 'Alderman Newington has asked to see me.' She swallowed to hide her own nervousness. 'You look tired,' she continued and took the serjeant's hand, turning it over carefully to examine it. The soldier, surprised, responded like a child.

'It hurts,' he murmured.

'It will hurt more,' Kathryn replied. 'If it goes septic, you will lose the hand.'

'What can I do?'

'Cleanse it with hot water. Infuse a little salt and a dash of wine mixed with vinegar. It will make you scream, but at least it will save your hand. Keep it covered with a bandage and repeat the process twice a day.'

'You are sure?' he asked, snatching Kathryn's letter from her hand. He held it upside down, pretending to read it.

'My name is Swinbrooke,' Kathryn added. 'I live in Ottemelle Lane. If your hand does not heal within three days, come and see me.'

The soldier gave a gap-toothed smile, his dull eyes sparkling into life.

'I will do that, Mistress.'

'Keep your dirty thoughts to yourself!' Thomasina interrupted. 'Mistress Swinbrooke is an apothecary and a doctor, not one of your camp followers!'

The soldier leered at Thomasina. 'It's you I'm after,' he teased. 'I like my women fat. Plenty to hold on to when the going gets rough!'

'I've pulled bigger things out of my nose!' Thomasina snapped back.

The soldier threw his head back and roared with laughter. 'I like them saucy,' he replied.

'Oliver, be careful!' one of his companions shouted. 'The Irishman expects these two.'

The serjeant quickly sobered up and stepped back. 'I thank you, Mistress. You had better hurry on.'

At the end of the passageway, through a milling crowd of frightened clerks, timorous burgesses and loud-mouthed soldiers, Kathryn met the alderman from her own ward, John Abchurch.

'Sir,' she cried out. 'Can you assist me?'

The plump little man turned. 'Mistress Swinbrooke. Of course. You should not be here.' He pulled his wool-lined cloak around him and edged closer. 'Troubled times, these. Faunte, God damn him, supporting the Lancastrians.'

'What will happen?'

'Faunte will lose his head or his balls. Probably both, and the city will have to pay a fine. Well'—Abchurch wetted his lips—'what do you want?'

'Alderman Newington wants to see me.'

'Come!'

Eager to escape the throng, Abchurch led them upstairs, along a quiet, deserted passageway, and tapped on a huge iron-barred door.

'Come in!'

Kathryn pushed the door open, even as Abchurch scuttled away like a rabbit. Inside the room was cool and, because the window shutters were open, bathed in sunlight, which made Kathryn blink after the dark passageway. Kathryn remembered her father's bringing her here years ago. Usually the chamber would be busy with merchants, aldermen, clerks and other officials of the city council, but now it was strangely deserted and the table at the far end empty.

'Over here, Mistress Swinbrooke!' a voice called out.

Kathryn looked towards the great fireplace. She saw four men sitting there. The nearest was an aged, venerable man; she glimpsed his gown of purple trimmed with costly fur. A clerk sat beside him, a writing-tray on his knee. On the other side of the fireplace she recognised Alderman John Newington, grey and lean as an ash pole. Beside him was a young man; Kathryn had the impression of long dark hair, hooded eyes and the sober bottle-green cloak, jacket and leggings of a soldier. All four rose as she walked tentatively towards them. Newington gestured at her to sit in a box-chair; a quilted stool stood beside it for Thomasina.

'Mistress Kathryn, you are welcome.'

Newington looked nervous, his bald head shimmering with sweat. His eyes were wary and his face lined with exhaustion. A merchant of some standing, Newington had probably been spared from the general purge of the city by the Yorkists because, as her father had once drily remarked, Newington could never make his mind up what day of the week it was, never mind which policy to follow. Kathryn smiled at him as he fidgeted with his fur-trimmed gown. She took another look at the soldier beside Newington; he was ugly, his face long and swarthy, the chin aggressive, the eyes hooded, the nose too sharp and his lips rather harsh and set. A close, secretive man. If Kathryn had met him in an alley-way she would have been wary, thinking he was some outlaw or wolf's-head.

'Mistress Swinbrooke?'

Kathryn turned to the old man and gasped as she suddenly realised his entire gown was purple. She had seen him in the abbey wearing the full vestments of Church and State, and Kathryn immediately curtsied to kiss the amethyst ring of Thomas Bourchier, Cardinal Archbishop of Canterbury. The Archbishop, despite his advanced years, helped Kathryn back to her seat. His face would have been forbidding for it was broad and fleshy, but his eyes were young and happy, as if he was genuinely pleased to be in the company of a young woman.

'It was good of you to come,' Bourchier murmured, his voice deep and rich-sounding. He tugged at the fleshy lobe of one ear. 'You must not be afeared. I am not here to excommunicate or interrogate.' His hand, vein-streaked and spotted with age, was warm and reassuring as he gripped Kathryn again. 'When I was a monk I knew your father. A good doctor, God rest him!' He looked with mock solemnity at Thomasina. 'And you must be physician Swinbrooke's maid? And Kathryn's nurse? I remember him once talking about you.'

Thomasina just simpered and for once kept her mouth shut.

'Sit down, please, sit down,' Newington fussed, gesturing at the chairs.

The little man beside the Archbishop scratched his nose with ink-stained fingers and glowered at the two women.

'Yes, sit down!' he snapped. 'Do you wish refreshment?'

Kathryn shook her head and smiled back at the fellow. She could tell from his dusty robe and ink-stained fingers, his writing-tray and ink-horn with quills resting on a small stool beside him, that he was probably one of the Archbishop's clerks, perhaps his principal one. A celibate who probably disliked women and resented her presence.

'Hush, Simon,' the Archbishop murmured. 'Not so harsh. We need Mistress Swinbrooke's help.'

Kathryn suddenly felt relieved that she was not here to answer questions about her father or the whereabouts of her missing husband. Bourchier leaned back in his chair, staring up at the hammer-beamed ceiling, gently rocking himself, his hands folded cherub-like across his broad girth. In contrast, his clerk Simon leaned forward, fingers clasped together, gazing at the ground, as if he refused to acknowledge Kathryn's presence. Newington fussed whilst beside him the soldier lolled in his seat, half-asleep. Kathryn gazed at him under half-closed eyelids; the fellow probably was dozing. She noticed his hands and face were dirty and his boots and leggings travel-stained.

'Master Newington.' She leaned forward. 'You asked to see me this morning?'

The alderman fussed with his robe. 'His Eminence the Cardinal Archbishop"—he bowed nervously at the prelate—'is well-known. Simon Luberon'—he flicked his hand at the secretarius—'is the Archbishop's principal clerk.' Newington smiled thinly. 'You know me. And this'—he half-turned to the soldier—'is Colum Murtagh, marshal in the King's household. And now . . .' Newington swallowed nervously.

'And now,' Murtagh suddenly spoke up, his speech low and tinged with a musical accent. 'And now,' he repeated, 'Keeper of the King's horses, stables and pastures in Kingsmead and Special Commissioner to the city.'

Kathryn stared at Murtagh. She knew Kingsmead, where the horses of the royal messengers were housed and fed. She'd heard the gossip of how, due to the recent civil war, both the small manor and its stables and outhouses had fallen into disrepair. Local farmers were even using the royal meadow to graze their own cattle. Murtagh looked as if he would soon put a stop to that. She heard Luberon angrily clicking his tongue.

'Why am I here?' she abruptly asked. 'Why am I summoned from my house?'

Newington laced his fingers together, licked his lips and glanced nervously at the Archbishop.

'Mistress Swinbrooke, there have been murders.'

Kathryn's blood chilled.

'Terrible murders, of pilgrims.'

Kathryn opened her mouth to speak.

'You have heard of them?' Luberon the clerk interrupted.

'I heard a rumour about a physician being poisoned in the Checker Board Tavern.'

'That's the fourth murder,' Bourchier interrupted. 'All were pilgrims, and all were poisoned.'

The Archbishop sighed. 'At first we did not notice, so many died due to the sweating sickness, but then we remembered a message pinned to the cathedral door.'

Bourchier turned and nodded at Luberon, who handed Kathryn a piece of parchment, greasy and thumb-marked.

'You can read?'

Kathryn ignored the jibe. "Of course, Master Clerk.'

She studied the scrawling letters. The message was cryptic:

Becket's tomb all dirt and crass
Radix malorum est Cupiditas.

Kathryn made a face. 'What does it mean, avarice is the root of all evil?'

'At first,' Bourchier answered, 'we thought it meant nothing, just a scrap of parchment pinned to the main door of the cathedral, but then a pattern began to emerge.' Bourchier leaned back in his chair. 'Other messages followed. The next read:

'A weaver to Canterbury his way did wend
And I to Heaven his soul I did send.

'Sure enough, a weaver from Evesham was poisoned in Burgate.' The Archbishop shrugged. 'Other messages and killings followed. A carpenter, a haberdasher, and then a doctor.' He stared at Kathryn. 'Before each murder, a message was nailed to the cathedral door, a doggerel verse, like the one you've just heard, naming the profession of the next victim.'

'And how does it concern me?'

'It doesn't.' Bourchier replied quietly. 'But can't you see, Mistress Kathryn, Becket's shrine is famous, it draws people from all over England as well as the rest of Europe.'

'And there's the profit,' Murtagh interrupted.

Bourchier shifted his heavy-lidded gaze to the soldier.

'Yes,' Newington admitted, 'there's the profit. Our shops, our stalls, our taverns, meeting-houses, indeed the whole city thrives on the pilgrims' trade. Can you imagine, Mistress Swinbrooke, if this news begins to spread?' Newington waved towards the window. 'People die like flies in battle or from disease, by accident or in a brawl in some tavern, but the poisoning of pilgrims is different. People come to Becket's shrine to be cured. Can you imagine what would happen if this mystery was fanned into a blaze of scandal? How a poisoner, a murderer was stalking the pilgrims of Canterbury?' He glared over his shoulder at the soldier. 'Matters are bad enough with the recent civil discord, though the King's victory in the west,' he added quickly, 'will soon put matters right.' He leaned forward. 'Mistress Swinbrooke, this poisoner has to be caught before other murders are committed.'

'You have other doctors, apothecaries.'

'There are a number of doctors in Canterbury and three apothecaries,' Newington answered. 'Though one of the latter is seriously ill.'

'Can't you see,' Luberon interrupted, 'why we have come to you? A woman!' The last word was spat out.

'Master Luberon, my father studied at the Saint Cosmos School of Medicine in Paris. Women doctors are recognised by the Guild in London. Queen Philippa of Hainault's physician was Cecilia of Oxford.' Kathryn trotted out the usual arguments espoused by her father. She shook her head wearily. 'I make no claims for greatness.' She appealed to the Archbishop. 'I am an apothecary; sometimes a leech; sometimes a doctor.'

'You should have been born a man,' Luberon jibed.

'In which case, Master Clerk, we have something in common!'

Behind her, Thomasina giggled. The soldier smiled, his face becoming young, quite attractive. Newington looked embarrassed, but the old Archbishop threw his head back and roared with laughter at Luberon's discomfort.

'Mistress Swinbrooke,' pleaded Newington before the puce-faced clerk could snap back. 'Can't you see our problem? Our poisoner knows Latin. He is an educated man.'

'How do you know he is a man?'

'Suffice to say we know he is. He is skilled in medicine. He must have access to potions and philtres. The very people you have listed, these,' he coughed, 'one of these doctors or apothecaries could be our murderer.'

'So could I!'

The Archbishop leaned forward in his chair. 'I don't think so.' He snapped his fingers at Luberon. 'You have the documents?'

'Yes, Your Grace.' The clerk handed Kathryn a small scroll wrapped in a piece of red silk. 'These are all the details we know.' Luberon preened himself. 'One of my clerks drew it up.'

Archbishop Bourchier suddenly stood up and gestured at the soldier. 'Master Murtagh here is an Irishman. He served Edward of York's father as a page, becoming marshal of the royal household and chief of the King's messengers. He now has responsibility for the royal stables at Kingsmead. He is also a Commissioner of the Peace in Canterbury. I asked the King for Murtagh's help in tracking down this murderer. I have chosen you to assist him.'

Kathryn looked at the Irishman, now staring blandly back at her. She caught a look she didn't like, cold, calculating, as if she were some mare in the market-place.

'You will be retained by this Corporation and by me,' Bourchier continued. 'On this, and any other matter, for sixty pounds a year, fifteen pounds delivered each quarter.'

Kathryn gasped in surprise, while behind her Thomasina fidgeted with excitement. She needed the money to buy stock for the shop, carry out the necessary repairs for the home, have her father's gravestone properly etched, and to hire a Jesus priest to sing chantry Masses.

'Do you accept?' the Archbishop snapped.

Kathryn nodded.

'Good!' Bourchier clapped his hands together. 'The

necessary letters will be delivered to your house. Let us keep the matter private and secret.'

'And if I fail?'

Bourchier smiled thinly. 'All murderers are caught,' he murmured. 'This one is no different. He is arrogant enough to over-reach himself.'

He took Kathryn by the hand and raised her to her feet. He quickly glanced to either side and Kathryn knew this cunning old priest had little trust in his companions. Indeed, the murderer could be anybody; Newington was a scholar, an educated man, as was Luberon. The Archbishop was warning her to be careful. Kathryn bowed her head and kissed his ring.

'I will do my best,' she said. 'Sirs, I bid you adieu.'

She walked back across the great hall, Thomasina trailing behind her. Outside the room they both leaned against the door. Kathryn's eyes widened.

'To be hired by the Corporation!' she whispered in mock pomposity. 'To be greeted by the Archbishop. Father would have been proud.'

'Of the money he would,' Thomasina answered. 'But he'd be more cunning than you.'

'What do you mean?'

Thomasina took her mistress by the elbow and walked her back to the top of the stairs.

'They call Bourchier a fox, and rightly so. He may be an Archbishop, but I wouldn't buy a horse from him. Luberon's a nasty piece of work, and Newington is probably frightened of his own farts.'

'What about the Irishman?'

Before Thomasina could answer, Kathryn heard her name being called. She turned. Murtagh now stood outside the hall, arms folded.

'Mistress Swinbrooke, a word.'

'You can have two,' Thomasina answered, 'if you promise to be civil.'

Murtagh walked towards them. He carried his head

high, moving like a cat, and Kathryn shivered. She was wary, frightened of this man with his dark face and his strange ways. The slight swagger, the way his knife and sword, pushed in rings round the broad belt, tapped against his leg reminded her and everyone else that he was a soldier, a killer, a cat amongst the pigeons. Yes, a cat, Kathryn thought as she remembered watching one stalk a bird in the garden just as slowly and carefully. Murtagh came closer, and Kathryn caught the smell of stale sweat and leather. She also noticed the dark rings round his eyes.

'You should sleep, Irishman. You have travelled far?'

'From Tewkesbury. It took three days. The King was insistent.'

Kathryn turned and went down the stairs, the Irishman following her.

'Have you read this?' she said, holding up the scroll.

'I am a soldier, not a clerk.'

'Can you read?' Thomasina jibed.

Murtagh grinned and suddenly seized the maid by the hand.

'And I suppose you can? It's rare to find a woman like you, Thomasina, who combines both beauty and brain.'

Thomasina pulled her hand away as they reached the bottom of the stairs.

'How do you know my name?' she snapped at him.

'Newington told me.'

'Are all Irishmen liars?'

'Perhaps, but if I called you a fat old hog,' he jested, 'would that be a truth or a lie?'

'You are a bog-trotter,' Thomasina snapped, 'with the arse hanging out of your pants. My old father said never trust Irishmen; they love fighting, drinking and wenching!'

'Thomasina!' Kathryn intervened. 'Master Murtagh, what do you know of these murders?'

Before Thomasina could object, Murtagh slipped beside Kathryn and led her out of the Guildhall down the steps. The sun shone fiercely and the din from the market in the High Street was deafening.

'Very little,' he replied. 'But here is not the time nor the place.' He moved closer and Kathryn glared at him.

'Where is the time and the place?' she asked warily.

'Mab's tits!' The Irishman caught her dislike and turned away. 'Mistress Kathryn, I mean no offence, but I am not one for taverns or cook-shops, and the house at Kingsmead is derelict.' He played with the hilt of his dagger. 'Look, if you invite me to supper, I will pay for whatever you cook.'

Kathryn blushed. 'I meant no offence,' she stammered. 'Of course you can come. The apothecary shop in Ottemelle Lane. An hour before sunset, as the bells toll for Vespers.'

The Irishman nodded and, turning on his heel, strode away.

'He's a bad bugger, that one,' Thomasina whispered. 'But I wager he's good in bed.'

'Thomasina, how do you know that?'

'You can tell by his legs,' her old nurse replied. 'Good and strong. Just like my third husband's. It's the first thing I noticed about him. He helped to carry my second husband's coffin down into church. I was walking behind and I thought, what a fine pair of legs, like tree trunks they were, and I was right!'

Kathryn smiled. She turned to go into the market but suddenly realised how tired she was, how little she had eaten and how relieved she was that there had been no talk about her husband. She was glad to have invited the Irishman to sup; whether she liked him or not, she and Murtagh were linked in hunting down a murderer who could be any one of the people milling in the market below.

Chapter 3

"Sir Thopas," as the murderer liked to call himself, stood in his Guild merchant's wool-lined cowl and hood just off the Buttermarket and watched the pilgrims stream through Newgate, across the lay folks' cemetery of Canterbury Cathedral, to visit Becket's shrine. He felt the small phial in his wallet as he waited for the merchants to come down Palace Street past St Alphege's Church, Turnagain Lane and into Sun Street. He had listened to their conversation in Burgate Lane Tavern the night before; just after noon, so one of them had remarked, they were to visit St Thomas à Becket's shrine, having paid for the considerable privilege of being given a special tour by a sub-prior of Christchurch.

The assassin leaned against the greystone house and looked up Burgate Street. He felt uncomfortable, not just because of the warm weather and stink but because of the presence of so many soldiers wearing the tabard of Edward of York. Then he grinned to himself. All of Canterbury was in chaos. The mayor was a traitor and the city council suspended; such confusion would mask his activities even further, and he had much to do. He gazed across where two beggars, crouching in the shadows of the boundary wall round the cathedral precincts, stretched out bony legs and rattled their copper dishes for pennies from the pilgrims. A group of scholars swept by shouting abuse at a butcher, who was trying to take a bull down to the baiting-post where it would be taunted and teased to make its humours run full and hot before it was slaughtered, for customers liked their beef full-blooded and rich. Thopas grinned; that's how he felt. He liked to choose his victim, seek him out, mark him down, draw up a subtle plan, plot the ambush, dispense death, then savor the grisly aftermath. He idly chanted two lines of a poem but stopped as a passing monk stared at him curiously.

Thopas heard loud talk and laughter and looked back up Sun Street. The merchants he had spied on the night before were approaching, dressed in their beaver hats, which they wore despite the heat. They had silver chains across their chests, buckles on their dusty boots, tawdry jewellery adorning throat and cuff. Near Newgate, the entrance to the abbey, they stopped. One of them produced a wineskin and they passed it around, talking and joking noisily. Thopas watched them cynically.

'They look more like a group of roistering youths,' he muttered, 'than pilgrims going to pray.' He narrowed his eyes. What's the use? he thought. Nobody could really believe in praying to a collection of dirty bones and pieces of filthy cloth. He studied the group, looking for his victim. Ah, there he was: fat and porky, chest and stomach stuck out like some pampered pigeon. His bald head and rubicund face were well-oiled, a fleshy nose jutted out over thick lips, and those eyes, hard as flint, never seemed at peace.

'Well, well,' Thopas muttered to himself. 'What doth it profit thee, merchant, if thou gain the whole world and suffer the loss of thy immortal soul?'

The murderer liked these quotations. He leaned against the house looking up at the sky. 'Fool,' he whispered, still quoting from the Scriptures, 'dost thou not know that this day, the demand has been made for thy soul?' He looked once more at his intended victim, whose fat lips were now round a wineskin. 'Drink deep,' he muttered, 'for the dark night cometh. You should have stored up riches in Heaven.'

He stared around once more, making sure no one was watching him. He became alert when the group of merchants fell quiet as one of them pointed through the cathedral gate at someone approaching them. Thopas strolled across Burgate, going behind the merchants, mixing with them so no one noticed his arrival. He had chosen this group because they were a disparate collection, wool traders from London, Rochester and Canterbury. Strangers, so happy and intent on their outing, they would hardly notice a stranger, thinking he, too, was a private visitor. The cathedral gates opened and a pale, thin-faced monk stepped out and talked to the leader of the group, quickly pocketing the small clinking purse offered to him. His skull-like face broke into a gap-toothed smile. He bowed and muttered a welcome, waving them forward. They were led across the lay-folk cemetery, the sub-prior pointing to two of the great towers of the cathedral. They stopped for a stoup of water at the fountain in the middle of the graveyard before going through the south porch of the cathedral. The sub-prior pointed to the statues of three knights above the door.

'The very ones who committed the dreadful murder of Becket,' he announced.

'Why are they in such a prominent place?' one of the merchants asked.

Again the gap-toothed smile from the monk. 'So no courtier or King,' he brayed, 'will ever again lay their hands on a Bishop or the riches of Holy Mother Church.'

He glared at the pilgrim merchants as if he suspected they had such an insidious design before leading the group into the nave. The murderer slipped quietly behind them. Other pilgrims had been halted because of this special visit and the lofty nave was deserted. The visitors were swept past various other monuments, the monk ignoring the latter with a flutter of his fingers, as if the greatness of any person buried there paled before the significance of Thomas à Becket. Thopas gazed up at the vastness of the building as the monk led them along the nave and up the broad stone steps to the choir. Just before they turned into the Martyr's transept, they were shown other wonders, such as the statue of Our Lady before which Becket was supposed to have prayed the evening he died. Nearby, on a small altar, the merchants were also shown the sword which the murderers had used to hack off the Archbishop's head.

'You may kiss this,' the monk announced.

The merchants did so, although Thopas made sure his lips never touched the rusting piece of metal.

After that they were led down to the crypt. The murderer trailed behind his intended victim, relishing the man's smell and swagger, the rubicund colour of his face and the self-importance he exuded. Soon, Thopas thought, you will be gone and nothing here will save you. For, as Master Chaucer says, "I dare well tell, though you walk here, your spirit's in hell." Thopas gazed round the cavernous crypt. It was all nonsense. He used to believe in the shrine, that's why he had brought his mother here. She, with her frail body, climbling like a dog up the pilgrim steps to pray before the shrine, begging for a cure for the tumour growing within her: for a while it had stopped, but then it abruptly increased.

'What's the matter?'

Thopas started and realised the rest of the group had gone deeper into the crypt. He felt a sense of panic, for he had always plotted never to be noticed, never to stand out. He peered through the gloom and breathed a sigh of relief. The merchant who was addressing him was his victim.

'Nothing,' Thopas replied, 'I was just overcome by the magnificence of it all.'

They rejoined the rest of the group, who were being shown other relics. First, the cleft skull of the Martyr, the forehead left bare so that they could kiss it, the rest covered in thick-plated silver. After that, other relics were displayed: the Archbishop's hair shirts, girdles and the strips of leather Becket had used to subdue his flesh. They were then taken back to the choir entrance where, on the north side, chest after chest was opened, containing the relics of other saints. The silver-lined boxes were full of skulls, jaw-bones, teeth, hands, fingers and entire arms, which the pilgrims were invited to kiss. Most of the merchants did so but a few drew back in disgust when the monk displayed a relic arm with the flesh still clinging to it.

The murderer sighed with relief as they were led up to the altar to view the cathedral's treasures: rich vessels and ornaments. They crossed into St Andrew's Chapel, which was stuffed full of precious vestments and golden candlesticks, including a pall of silk and a napkin with spots of real blood on its dingy surface.

'These were used,' the monk announced, 'to cover the dead Archbishop's body. Now,' the monk continued triumphantly, 'the climax of your visit.'

He led them up another flight of steps to Becket's tomb in Trinity Chapel. This was dominated by a figure of the saint gilded and adorned with many jewels. The merchants stood back in awe; even they, with their wealth and coffers full of gold, gazed in a mixture of envy and admiration at the beauty of the statue.

The sub-prior climbed a ladder and, using a pulley, raised a wooden case which kept the shrine hidden from the vulgar gaze of the masses. Even Thopas, who believed in nothing and had seen the treasures many times before, gasped in admiration. The entire shrine was covered in gold plate and studded with very large rare jewels which caught the light and dazzled the eye. Some of the jewels were bigger than a goose's egg, the most brilliant being the Regal of France, which shone like a burst of fire. The merchants were allowed to gaze in silent awe at this gorgeous display of wealth before the screen was lowered and they were taken to a nearby sacristry. Here, they knelt in worship as a box covered in black leather was produced and opened to reveal a few fragments of dirty linen.

'These,' the monk announced, 'are what our Martyr would use to wipe the perspiration off his face and the runnings from his nose.'

The merchants just stared speechlessly. A few turned away, slightly revolted. The box was closed and a lay brother entered carrying a tray of wine-cups and plates of wafers.

Thopas now worked himself forward to the front of the group, the small phial in his left hand, whilst the merchants chattered and dug deep in their purses for coins to put in the collection plate. Making use of the darkened room, Thopas distributed the wine. He made sure he served his victim last and, as he handed the cup over, took advantage of the general hubbub of conversation to drop the poisoned powder into the cup, swirling the wine gently, allowing it to dissolve. Then he stood silent and, for a few seconds, watched his victim drink his death before stepping back into the shadows and fleeing like a ghost from the cathedral.

At her house in Ottemelle Lane, Kathryn Swinbrooke sat in her small writing-chamber. She was pretending to work whilst the red-faced, sweating Thomasina laboured in the kitchen preparing a meal. Thomasina quietly cursed all men, particularly bog-trotting Irishmen who, she told in a loud whisper to Agnes, would eat them out of house and home before ravishing them in their beds.

'Chance it would be a fine thing,' Kathryn murmured with a half-smile. She listened to Thomasina's lurid description, interspersed by Agnes's noisy gasps, of what Irish mercenaries would do if any hapless maid fell into their brutal, coarse hands.

'Oh, yes,' Thomasina bellowed, knowing full well her voice would carry to her mistress's writing-chamber, 'I have heard stories about Edward of York's mercenaries.' She lowered her voice to a whisper which Kathryn thought could be heard in the Guildhall. 'Listen! They take a maid, strip her ever so slowly and lash her hands above her head to a post. They stand around drinking and then they do the most dreadful things.'

'Such as?' Agnes squeaked hopefully.

Now Thomasina's voice fell to a real whisper as she regaled the girl with every juicy tidbit of sexual scandal she had heard in her long and varied life. Kathryn grinned and looked down at the table. Someone had said Thomasina's mouth was as big as a drain and as filthy, but Kathryn knew her to have a heart of gold. Nevertheless, her nurse's constant references to Irishmen reminded Kathryn of what had occurred earlier in the day. The mystery behind that meeting; the prospect of greater income; the grubby menace of that deserted Guildhall thronged with soldiers. Bourchier's cunning eyes in his red vein-streaked face; Luberon, nasty as a wasp; Newington, so frightened he looked as if he would faint. And that silent, swaggering soldier with his strange eyes and mocking air of menace.

Kathryn played with the cap of her ink-horn. Was she frightened of Murtagh? 'No, no,' she whispered to the darkness. She thought again. Yes, she was, and in the coldness of her heart she cursed her husband. She had to face the truth Thomasina constantly pushed before her. She was frightened, wary of men, and who could blame her? Alexander Wyville, so gentle, so caring, so assiduous in his courtship. She remembered her wedding night, the sweetness and passion of those early days. Then the truth.

Alexander drunk, his face a twisted mask of hatred as he dredged up from his own dark soul the wrongs and injuries done by a cruel step-father. His resentment at the lack of a proper education. His failure to become a truly prosperous merchant. He would stand in their bedchamber, squirting the wineskin into his mouth as he repeated once again his litany of hate.

At first Kathryn thought it was a passing mood. She had seen her own father become drunk and maudlin, but he would relax and tell jokes about a certain friar. Alexander was different. When he was drunk, he lived in his own dark dungeon. When Kathryn had tried to intervene, the real nightmare had begun, for Alexander came to see her as the living personification of all that he thought he deserved and had lost. He turned violent: a fist to her face, a blow to her stomach; sometimes kicking and lashing her as if he were some alley brawler. In the morning when he was sober he would be contrite, but Kathryn soon realised she had married two, not one man.

She closed her eyes and tried to listen to Agnes's shrieks of delicious outrage. She must not think of Alexander. If she did, her father's face would come back, swimming through her memories. She took a deep breath, leaned against the high-backed chair and tried to think of other matters. Should she change her dress before the Irishman arrived? She felt a tingle of excitement in her stomach. After all, he was the King's Commissioner, a member of the King's personal chamber: a trusted squire whom even the cardinal bishop treated with respect. Kathryn smelt the first savoury tang of the meat Thomasina was roasting and shook her head. No, she would give the Irishman a good meal, and that was enough.

Kathryn stared at the small roll of parchment, picked it up and carefully undid its ribbon of silk. At first she found it difficult to follow the cramped, clerkly hand, for her mind was distracted and Thomasina was still bellowing about the lustful intents of Irish bog-trotters.

'Oh, shut up, Thomasina,' Kathryn whispered to herself.

She began reading once again, and despite the official, bureaucratic tone of the clerk, the real menace of what she was facing began to emerge.

A true and accurate account of the horrible murders committed in the city of Canterbury against pilgrims visiting the Blessed Martyr's shrine. The first such felony was committed on April 5th. Aylward of Evesham, a weaver, together with other members of that town, visited the shrine to supplicate before the Martyr's tomb. Aylward was a good man, of yeoman stock, careful and sober in his ways. The mayor and jury of that town had sworn an oath that Aylward was a loyal citizen and faithful subject of the King. He was well-liked and respected and had no enemies or business rivals. The pilgrims from Evesham arrived in Canterbury on Tuesday and visited the shrine late on Wednesday morning. They joined the other pilgrims and nothing untoward was noticed except that Gervase, a companion of the said Aylward, claimed that after they left the cathedral enclosure, they were approached by a water-seller. The fellow was old, with a hood pulled well over his head. He offered the townsfolk of Evesham free stoups of cold water, drawn fresh from a nearby well. The water-seller explained he did this as an act of mercy. The pilgrims, over-joyed at such generosity, were each offered a cup of water from the fellow's barrel. The water-seller teased Aylward, saying he looked their leader and, to quote the words of the Gospel, 'The first would be last and the last would be first.' So Aylward was served after them all. The water-seller disappeared and the pilgrims were going back to their tavern in Westgate when Aylward fell to the ground in a dead swoon and expired shortly afterwards. A local physician, John Talbot, was summoned by the alderman of the ward. He pronounced Aylward dead, God assoil him, and said that his death was due to a potent poison. The pilgrims from Evesham swore no suspicion could fall on any of their group. The Corpo-

ration ordered a search for this mysterious water-seller, but no trace of him has been found.

The second murder occurred two weeks later. Very little evidence exists except that the victim, Osbert Obidiah, a carpenter from a village outside Maidstone, was found dead in an alley-way off Burgate. The blackness of his mouth and tongue loudly proclaimed that he had died of no sudden seizure but that he, too, had been horribly poisoned.

The third death followed soon afterwards. Ranulf Floriack, a haberdasher and pilgrim from Acton Burnley, was supping with other pilgrims in the Winged Horse Tavern in Pissboil Alley. The pilgrims were of poor means and had ordered cups of watered wine and bowls of onion soup, for which the tavern was famous. Shortly after finishing his bowl, Ranulf was taken violently ill with cramps in his stomach and, despite the consolation and help given by his companions, expired in the stable-yard behind the tavern. Again no suspicions fell upon his companions, so questions were asked of the taverner. Apparently Ranulf had been murdered with arsenic, the same potion used against Osbert. A search was made of the tavern; no poisons or potions found there. But the landlord confessed all was not well.

'You see,' he explained, 'I hire a number of pot-boys and slatterns during the pilgrim season. My customers are many, often hungry, so my kitchens are busier than any beehive. Apparently, for a few minutes, whilst the pilgrims from Acton Burnley were being served, one of the slatterns noticed a servant working in the tavern whom she had never seen before. He had long, greasy hair, a dirty apron, and she was sure he served the pilgrim group.'

The girl in question had also been interrogated, but all she could report was glimpsing a servitor, his face blackened with dirt and grease, his hair long and straggly, rather tall, pushing through the group towards the pilgrims. She had not seen him previously, nor since.

The fourth murder was more recent, a few days ago; in fact, just before the news of the King's victory at Tewkesbury reached the city. Robert Clerkenwell, a physician from London, had been poisoned in the Checker Board Tavern in Burgate near the stocks. He had been drinking Rhenish wine when suddenly he dropped, as if from a seizure, death being almost instantaneous. Geoffrey Cotterell, a physician . . .

Kathryn looked up and pulled a face. She knew Cotterell. A busy, nasty man who served the rich and didn't give a fig for anyone else. Her father always claimed he was a charlatan and quietly mocked Cotterell's supercilious air and ostentatious dress. Kathryn went back to the manuscript.

. . . Cotterell [the clerk continued] had been in the 'vicinity' [Kathryn took a pen and underlined this]. He examined the dead physician and said the skin was so cold and clammy, he must have been poisoned with a strong infusion of some subtle poison such as foxglove, which would stop the heart and lead to sudden death. Once again the pilgrims were interrogated. A search made of their possessions proved fruitless, and no blame could be attached to them. A perfunctory search of the Checker Board Tavern was also made and, strange upon strange, a scullion similar to the one glimpsed in the Winged Horse had been seen serving the dead physician and his companions.

The manuscript abruptly ended there. Kathryn read it once again, quietly mouthing the words. She then rose and went into the kitchen, rather concerned because of the silence there. Thomasina and Agnes had gone into the garden and were collecting herbs. Now Agnes was stripping them of their leaves and stems whilst Thomasina was crushing the herbs with a small wooden mortar and pestle. Kathryn leaned against the door lintel and watched them. Agnes, round-eyed, could hardly concentrate on what she was doing but kept staring at Thomasina, perched on the corner of the small garden wall, still regaling the young maid with the sexual habits of Irish mercenaries. Kathryn stretched, quietly vowing she would buy a better chair, perhaps one cushioned and quilted. She took a pewter cup and filled it with water from a pitcher and stood enjoying the smells from the meat slowly roasting over the fire. Absent-mindedly she walked back to her chamber, sipping from the cup. The Irishman would undoubtedly ask questions, but so far, what could she say? The whole business troubled her and touched upon memories . . . something she had either read, or had her father told her? She paused at the entrance to her writing-office. How did that doggerel verse run?

Becket's tomb all dirt and crass,
Radix malorem est Cupiditas.

Something about the verses stirred her memory. And why did the assassin choose his victim by profession? She remembered the verse.

A weaver to Canterbury his way did wend,
And to Heaven his soul I did send.

Kathryn shook her head and sat down at the table. How would her father have resolved this problem? Here, in this office, she felt his presence draw closer, as if he were standing by the chair, leaning over her.

'Always remember, Kathryn,' he used to say, 'we physicians know nothing. If you have a sore throat, I can give you a fusion of honey and herbs. I know it will help, but I cannot explain why. If you break your arm, I can set it into a splint; usually it heals but I can't explain why. A good physician can only watch, study and draw conclusions. Look at the evidence. A man's eyes, the state of his nails and hair, the way he sits, the manner of his breathing.'

Kathryn stared down at the clerk's memorandum. Perhaps she should apply the same rules to this. She took up a piece of parchment and smoothed it out. So far, what could she say?

Four men had been murdered, all poisoned. At least two potions had been used: foxglove and arsenic. There was no apparent motive, no evidence linking the assassin with his victim. All had been pilgrims at Canterbury; thus the writer of the anonymous doggerels apparently hated the shrine, saw it as mummery and was bent on a twisted revenge against it and the whole idea of pilgrimage. Lastly, he chose his victims by profession. Why?

Kathryn fell into a day-dream. She half-heard Thomasina and Agnes come back into the house. The smells from the kitchen became more tantalising as Kathryn stared down at what she had written. She picked up the quill, dipped it into the green ink and carefully wrote:

'The murderer—a man? Someone who could disguise himself as a menial servant and move unnoticed amongst the crowd. Yet he must be intelligent, educated and fairly prosperous. He could write doggerel verses, knew a great deal about poisons and had access to a ready supply.' Kathryn stopped and underlined this, idly twisting the jewelled bangle on her wrist as it sparkled in the light. There could only be one conclusion: the poisoner must be either an apothecary or a doctor.

Kathryn went back and studied the details of the last death, the doctor's, Robert Clerkenwell, at the Checker Board Tavern. He had been drinking Rhenish wine. This was white and clear. Its sharp taste would hide the tang of foxglove, and since this poison came in crushed white powder, it would dissolve in only a few seconds. Like any apothecary, Kathryn knew that foxglove could be used in minute doses to strengthen a sickly heart, but that in larger quantities it would lead to seizure and death. Only a trained physician or apothecary would know that foxglove has to be left to dissolve for a few seconds before it could be drunk. She put down the pen. The poisoner, she reflected, must be someone who lived in or near Canterbury, someone who knew the streets and alleyways, who could disappear, hide and re-emerge in a different disguise. But why? Why the verses? Why the hatred for the shrine? Kathryn jumped, startled as she heard a knock at the door and the harsh voice of Colum Murtagh demanding entrance.

Chapter 4

Colum came just inside the door, moving restlessly from foot to foot. Thomasina stood next to him, holding a ladling spoon whilst Agnes peeped from behind her as if the Irishman had come to plunder and rape. Kathryn hurried towards him.

'Master Murtagh, you are most welcome.'

The Irishman looked at her and Kathryn suddenly felt embarrassed. Murtagh had taken pains to prepare himself for the visit. Someone had cut his hair, he had shaved and washed, and his sun-tanned face now had a clean, sharp, polished look. He had also changed his dress: a crisp linen shirt under a dark velvet jacket with silver buttons on the sleeves and fresh hose of brown fustian pushed into shining black riding-boots. He still wore his great leather war belt and from a brass ring hung sword and dagger in their sheaths. His fingers kept touching these, as if he were reassuring himself that all was well. Kathryn waved him to the table now laid out for the meal.

'Master Murtagh,' she repeated, 'you are most welcome.'

He coughed and walked towards her, his hand going inside his jerkin. He pulled out a piece of long blue silk and almost pushed it at Kathryn.

'This is for you, Mistress.'

His hand went down to his dagger as if he expected Kathryn to throw the present back. Kathryn unrolled the gift, enjoying the feel of its silkiness on her hands.

'It's a scarf,' Colum announced abruptly, staring round the kitchen. 'It's a long time, Mistress, since anyone invited me to eat in their house.'

'Small wonder,' whispered Thomasina.

Kathryn folded the silk carefully, ignoring the oohs and aahs of Agnes.

'Someone else's property,' Thomasina mumbled.

Kathryn glared at her maid and stroked the silk gently. 'It's beautiful.' She was about to say 'Master Murtagh' when the Irishman stepped closer, touching her gently on the back of her hand.

'Colum, my name's Colum.'

'And she,' Thomasina interrupted surlily, 'Is Mistress Swinbrooke.'

Kathryn grinned and told Agnes to take the present to her chamber. Colum relaxed, no longer the veteran soldier but rather embarrassed and shy. He dug inside his jacket again and brought out a silver bangle, a fine strip of pure silver thickened at each edge, and before Thomasina could object, Colum strode over and clasped it gently round her pudgy wrist.

'And that's for you,' he murmured.

Thomasina, for once, was lost for words. She opened her mouth to protest, caught Kathryn's warning glance and stomped back to the fire, muttering that the food would be spoilt.

The meal was a strange affair. Thomasina was an excellent cook, but it had been a long time since Kathryn had entertained anyone. Naturally, Thomasina and Agnes had laid places for themselves, determined to watch the Irishman and criticise his every move. At first, the conversation was desultory: the weather, the price of crops, interspersed by Colum's direct questions about Canterbury, its city, buildings, people and customs. He rarely looked at Kathryn but directed most of his questions at Thomasina or Agnes. Kathryn let the conversation flow as she discreetly studied the Irishman. At first she thought he was a common soldier, yet, although he ate hungrily, he complimented Thomasina on her cooking and cut his meat and used his napkin like any courtier. Kathryn bit her lip and vowed not to make such hasty judgements. The Irishman was the King's marshal, and he had been entrusted with special tasks, so he must be acquainted with courtly etiquette as well as the rules of war.

At last the meal ended. Agnes, who had drunk rather deeply, was heavy-eyed with sleep. Kathryn told her to retire, leaving Thomasina to clear the table. As she was removing dishes, trenchers, bowls and plates and taking them into the scullery, the Irishman pushed back his chair and sipped slowly from the wine goblet. His dark, hooded eyes caught and held Kathryn's.

'You like the silk, Mistress Swinbrooke?'

'My name is Kathryn, and yes, I did. It was most courteous of you.'

The Irishman smiled, as if it was a matter of little importance. Kathryn would have loved to have asked him directly. Had he bought the gifts, or were they plunder from some pillaged house or the tents of an enemy?

'I bought both in London,' he said quietly, as if reading her mind. 'I am not a thief, Kathryn, and in Ireland a gift is a pledge of friendship. What I have, I hold.' His voice became hard. 'And what I hold is mine.'

Kathryn looked away. She just hoped Murtagh wouldn't detect the faint blush of embarrassment on her neck and cheeks.

'Why was I chosen?' she asked sharply.

Colum pulled a face. 'Why not? I am told you have a reputation for being a fine doctor. In fact, a physician with a special skill for herbs and potions. Most doctors I have met are quacks or charlatans.'

'It might have been easier to have chosen a man.'

Colum put the wine-cup back on the table and leaned forward.

'Newington recommended you. I made enquiries, and although that proud clerk Luberon is a pompous little prig and Bourchier is a priest, they both confirmed the alderman's comments. And before you ask, Kathryn, I have no difficulty in working with a woman physician. In Ireland all healers are wise women.' His glance fell away, then he looked up and grinned. 'Yet they are not as comely as you.'

Kathryn smiled back.

'And how long have you been out of Ireland, Colum?'

Murtagh became defensive. 'Fifteen years.'

'And you have been a royal marshal and messenger ever since?'

Colum drew in his breath. 'I was a member of the household of the present King's father.' He shrugged. 'You know the way it is. I had a skill for horses.'

He moved the wine-cup round the table. Kathryn noticed how strong his brown stubby fingers were. She saw their muscles tense and knew the Irishman did not want to open the baggage of his past.

'So now you are the Keeper of the royal stables at Kingsmead?'

Colum laughed drily. 'Stables!' he exclaimed. 'The manor-house is derelict, the stables cracked and dirty. The meadows over-grown, fences broken down. The place is more like a wasteland than anything else!'

'And this task of trapping the murderer?'

Colum leaned back in his chair. 'You know as much as I do. You see,' he continued briskly, 'His Majesty the King's attitude towards Canterbury is that of a father who wishes to chastise a favoured child. Canterbury, or rather its mayor, Nicholas Faunte, declared for Lancaster. Faunte is to be hunted down, and when he is captured, he will hang. The Corporation must be punished, yet Becket's tomb is a jewel in the crown. The King, the Archbishop, the monks of the cathedral wish it protected and cannot allow some assassin to strike like the Angel of Death whenever he so wishes.'

'What makes you think it's a man?' Kathryn interrupted. 'It might well be a woman.' She leaned her arms on the table. 'You have no proof that it's not me.'

Colum flicked a crumb of bread from the table-cloth.

'We have discussed this. You're no murderer, Mistress. Moreover, what witnesses we have talk of a man. However, you do accept that the murderer is a physician?'

Kathryn nodded. 'Only a physician or a skilled herbalist,' she replied, 'would know how to use arsenic or foxglove. Such poisons are expensive, so our assassin is a man of means with a ready provision of such potions. He also knows Canterbury well, so he is able to slip through sideways and alley-ways whenever he wishes. He can change his appearance, and the doggerel verses illustrate he has some learning. So, yes, Colum, our assassin is probably a physician. But who he is and why he kills is a mystery.'

Colum tapped his chin with his fingers. 'Yes,' he replied softly. He stopped and looked round. 'So where is the ever-watchful Thomasina?'

'I'm in the scullery, Irishman!' Kathryn's maid retorted loudly. 'And, believe me, I can hear your every word!'

Kathryn grinned. Colum threw a smile towards the scullery door and without asking picked up the pewter jug of wine and filled both his cup and Kathryn's to the brim.

'In vino veritas,' he murmured. 'In wine truth, Mistress Swinbrooke. Tell me what makes a man hate a shrine so much he will commit murder after murder as a blind act of revenge?' He stared narrowly at Kathryn. 'People kill for two reasons.' He picked up the wine-cup and stared at it. 'They kill because they are paid; perhaps I am one of those. Soldiers in battle, hacking and hewing, fighting for a cause they don't really believe in except it will profit them, put silver in their purses, food in their bellies and a roof over their heads. At Tewkesbury, however, the great ones fought for something else, not just for power and wealth but out of hate.' He looked sharply at Kathryn. 'I was there at the end when the Lancastrian lords surrendered in the abbey. You have heard the story?'

Kathryn shook her head.

'They dragged them out,' Colum continued. 'No longer great lords but battered and bruised men. The King's brother, Richard of Gloucester, sat in a great chair before the abbey gates and judged them guilty of treason. They were hustled down to the nearby market-place and I fell asleep that night to the sound of the executioner's axe striking heads from shoulders.'

Kathryn watched him carefully. The wine had loosened his tongue, for Colum was talking as if there were no one there. She also noticed how quiet Thomasina in the scullery had become.

'People kill,' Colum said quietly, 'because they like it. And why do they like it? Because they hate. And what is hate but love grown cold?' He moved suddenly. The wine slopped onto his hose and he wiped it angrily away. He faced Kathryn squarely. 'Our murderer is someone who hates the shrine because he was disappointed by it. A physician who once placed great trust in it but now holds it responsible for some terrible event. Don't you agree, Mistress Swinbrooke?'

'Why did you fight?' she asked abruptly.

The Irishman smiled but his eyes remained hard. Kathryn looked away. She would have to be careful with this man. Was he like Alexander? Did he have a demon in his soul which would surface when the wine flowed and beat in his head?

'I fought,' he grated, 'because I had to, because I was paid. I would like to lie, Kathryn, to say I was only a messenger, but at the beginning of one battle I killed a man, an enemy scout who tried to surprise me. He came running at me. I moved my horse and brought my sword down to catch him neatly between shoulder and neck.' He licked his lips. 'I can still see his face,' he murmured, 'that terrible, surprised look.' Colum blinked and stared around as if he realised he had said too much. 'It could have been someone you knew.'

Kathryn caught the challenge in his question. 'You mean my husband?'

'Alexander Wyville was a Lancastrian.'

Kathryn refused to be drawn. 'My husband died long before any battle,' she replied in a half-whisper.

'Do you know if he's dead?'

Now Kathryn stared at the wine in her own cup.

'I don't know. I do not wish to talk about it.' She felt a chill run down her back. What could she say?

Colum studied her carefully. Throughout the meal Kathryn had maintained her poise, but he sensed her husband's disappearance was a chink in the armour of this rather austere, self-contained woman. Oh, she had smiled and laughed, she had eaten and drunk, but until now, never once had she made any movement, given any sign, of what she really felt.

Colum rose and stretched, slapping his thigh gently, easing the belt round his stomach.

'You have a garden, Mistress Swinbrooke?'

Kathryn stared at him. Was he baiting her? Did he know more than he had revealed? The Irishman smiled apologetically.

'It's warm,' he murmured. 'I wondered if the night air would refresh both of us.'

Kathryn realized she was being churlish, and smiled. She led Colum out into the warm velvet darkness. They stood on the raised pavement just beyond the porch. Kathryn was glad it was dark. In the silver moonlight she could discern the herb-banks, the white flowers picking up the light, but beyond lay the small dark orchard, the source of her secret nightmare. Colum pointed at the herbs.

'You grow your own produce?'

'Only some,' Kathryn answered. 'Others I buy, but the price is high and soldiers on the road send prices even higher.'

Colum smiled wolfishly and looked up. 'I'm glad the war's over,' he said. 'And I am free of camp and court.'

'So you think it's ended?'

'Edward the Fourth, God bless him, will keep what is his. You have heard the news?'

Kathryn shook her head.

'The Lancastrians are finished. Margaret of Anjou is captured and her son was killed at Tewkesbury.'

'And the old King?'

'Ah, that's the news. He died in the Tower.'

Kathryn stared up at the sky, trying to conceal her fear. The Irishman was telling her that the Lancastrian King had been murdered. The Lord's anointed, old Henry VI, had been assassinated in that narrow prison, probably by men like the one standing next to her.

'Do you think our murderer has a herb garden?'

'He must have,' she answered. 'But there's something else.'

Colum turned and faced her. 'What do you mean?'

'I accept this assassin in the shadows is a physician, a man who knows both Canterbury and herbs well and cherishes a great grudge against the shrine. Yet those doggerel verses remind me of something. And why does he choose his victims by their profession? Why not just kill indiscriminately? Can you answer that, Master Murtagh?'

Colum was about to reply when Thomasina came bustling through the door.

'Mistress! Mistress! Come quickly!'

Kathryn followed her back into the kitchen. The table had now been cleared, the fire dampened. Thomasina had even put out Kathryn's herb cutting board, with its sharp knife ready for business the next morning.

'Thomasina, what is it?'

Her maid handed over a small square piece of parchment. Kathryn took it and went across to the table. Even as she unfolded and read it in the light of the candle, her heart beat a little quicker. The message ran the same: 'Where is Alexander Wyville? Where is your husband? Murder is a felony and felons hang.' Beside the usual rudely scrawled words was a gibbet with a caricature of a woman hanging from the rope. Kathryn felt a surge of rage. Crackling the piece of parchment in her hand, she tossed it furiously into the flames.

'Mistress, what is it?'

'Nothing, Thomasina. Leave me alone.'

Kathryn's face was white and drawn. Her eyes, dark pools of anxiety, reminded Thomasina of how Kathryn used to look after those dreadful nightly quarrels with her husband. Kathryn blinked and forced a smile.

'Thomasina, I'm sorry, but please, go to bed. I will be well.'

'Not while he's here!' Thomasina flung her hand out at Colum, who was watching Kathryn curiously.

'Your mistress is safe with me,' he snarled. 'Which is more than I can say for yourself! Now go, woman!'

Thomasina glared at Kathryn, who nodded, and the maid, her face red with anger, backed out, throwing one last cautionary look at her mistress. Kathryn heard her go down the passageway and slowly climb the wooden stairs to her bedchamber; she stood staring into the flames turning that hateful note to powdery ash. Who was it, she wondered, who sent such malicious messages? Where was her husband? What had happened in the garden? And was her father's last confession true? Should she go back and talk to Father Cuthbert? Yes, perhaps it was time. Colum touched her hand.

'Kathryn, what is the matter? Mistress, your hand is cold. It's like ice.'

Kathryn glared up at him. 'Let go of my hand, Irishman!'

Colum squeezed it tightly.

'Irishman, let go of my hand! Believe me, soldier, there are more ways of killing a man than with dagger, sword or spear! Ground glass in wine would turn the hardest man's belly to a bloody pulp!'

Colum released her fingers and stepped back. Kathryn continued to glare at him. What in God's name, she wondered, was he doing here with his sword-belt, his dagger and his sword? She felt tired and slightly light-headed and walked over to her father's great high-backed chair before the hearth. She sat down and stared into the fire. What had gone wrong? Life had once seemed so happy. She heard a movement beside her.

'You'd better go,' she said, not shifting her gaze. 'You'd best go now.'

Kathryn heard the Irishman walk away and waited for the door to open and shut. She closed her eyes and forced back the tears. She had been too harsh with Thomasina. She hadn't even asked how the message had come, and the Irishman had only meant well. She heard Murtagh return and looked up. He had put his cloak on but he also held two wine-cups. He thrust one at her.

'Drink, woman. For God's sake, drink. Anyone can see you're frightened.'

He squatted down beside her and stared at the dying embers of the fire as if he wished he could pluck the message out and read what had startled this enigmatic woman.

'I meant well,' he said. 'God save you, Mistress, I did. But what affects you now affects me. Was that message about the murders?'

'No, it wasn't.'

'Then what could frighten you so much?'

'It's my business.'

'Can I help?'

Kathryn sipped from the wine and looked at him. He looks like a boy, she thought, open-faced and clear-eyed. Perhaps he could help. Then she remembered Alexander could also look like that, in the morning after he had shaved, washed and cleaned his mouth, as if purifying himself of the demons from the night before. She looked away and steeled herself. She would have loved to have screamed at Colum to get out, to leave her alone. She recalled the gibbet on the letter, the menacing words, and realised she might need, if not this man's friendship, then at least his help. But not now! She could not open her heart like some chattering child in front of a stranger.

'You are badly frightened, Mistress,' he repeated.

Kathryn sighed. 'Yes, Colum. You understand the word "fear"?'

The Irishman half-sighed and backed away.

'When I was a young boy,' he began softly, 'ten or eleven summers old, I was a page, really a lackey, at the manor of Gowran, a great sprawling place in the country-side near Dublin. You have been to Ireland?'

Kathryn shook her head.

'A wild greenness,' Colum continued. 'Harsh land, bogs, swamps, forests, but also the most beautiful pasture land, rich and yielding; bubbling streams, meadows full of flowers. The Master of Gowran owned land like this and I was being trained in his household. Now there was a priest there, a worldly man. All he lived for was hunting. He loved his dogs and horses more than his parishioners. He said the quickest Mass in Christendom and seemed little concerned with matters of his soul. He drank and wenched and didn't give a fig for God or man. He was small, fat-bellied, red-faced and had the coldest eyes I have ever seen. He was called the Dog Priest because of his hounds.' Colum paused and drew his cloak more firmly about him. 'I hated this man, his very touch made my skin crawl. One day he went out hunting, suffered a seizure and fell dead on the spot.' Colum stared into the dying flames of the fire. 'God knows why, but the Master of Gowran refused to have him laid to rest in the church. Instead he was buried on the brow of a hill under a cairn of stones.' Colum paused and listened to the sounds of the night from the street outside.

'Continue, Colum.'

'The priest was buried at night. I remember the torch-lit procession, his coffin on a high-wheeled cart, and around it, men from the manor carrying torches. We went to the top of a hill. A terrible wind whipped our faces and we struggled to keep the torches alight. We tried to sing the "De Profundis," but the words died on our lips. The sky became overcast. The only sound was the horrible howling of a dog baying at the night skies.' Colum stopped to control those childhood terrors which had never left his soul. 'We reached the top of the hill,' he continued. 'The coffin was lowered into the ground and covered with earth; then the peasants rolled huge boulders on top. The Master tried to say some words.' Murtagh looked at Kathryn. 'There was no priest. The clouds massed, whipped up by the wind. The rain began to fall, and all the time that terrible howling continued, so we made a sign of the cross, the horses were hitched and we left that dreadful hill.' Colum grasped Kathryn by the wrist. 'As we descended that hill, the rains stopped, the storm died and the Master had the sconce torches re-lit. I was sitting beside the driver on a cart, and suddenly, along the moonlit trackway, we saw a figure walking before us. He didn't turn or stop. I thought it was someone who had left the funeral service early. The carter drew alongside him. I called out, "Good evening, stranger." Colum's grip on Kathryn's smooth wrist tightened. 'You must believe me, Mistress. That hooded, cowled figure turned and the white, ugly face of the Dog Priest, the very man we had just buried, was grinning at me.' Murtagh gazed into the fire and then back at Kathryn. 'Oh, Mistress Swinbrooke,' he murmured, 'I screamed and fell into a swoon. When I awoke I was back in the manor and the wife of the Master was bending over me, forcing wine between my lips. She asked me what had happened, and being a child, I told her. She looked troubled but shook her head; she said it was a phantasm and warned me to tell no one else.'

'And did you?' Kathryn asked.

'No. I kept my thoughts to myself, but I knew others had seen him. Dreadful things began to happen in the area. The Master of Gowran had new walls built; stronger doors, which were bolted at night.' Murtagh paused and drew a deep breath. 'Oh, I heard the old women tell about the Deargdul. Do you know who they are?'

Kathryn shook her head, though Colum noticed how tense and watchful she had become.

'It's Gaelic,' Colum said. 'Roughly translated, it means the "drinkers of blood". ' Colum saw Kathryn shudder. 'Two years later,' he continued, 'I left Gowran to serve as a squire within the Pale of Dublin, but I wanted to confront my fears. So one afternoon, I went back up that lonely hill to the Dog Priest's grave.'

'And what did you find?'

'The stones were overturned,' Colum whispered. 'I later discovered that this had happened almost immediately after the Dog Priest's funeral.'

'And the grave?'

'A dusty, empty pit.'

Kathryn smiled and glanced at Murtagh.

'An old Irish trick,' she said, 'to replace one fear with another.' She crossed her arms and shivered. 'A frightening story.'

Colum thought of the Hounds of Ulster and their lifelong vendetta against him. 'I suppose I spoke in parables,' he replied. 'I have fears which spring out from my past. I suspect the same is true of you, Mistress Swinbrooke.' He tapped her on the wrist and this time she did not flinch. 'But now I must leave you.' He nodded at the ceiling. 'I am sure Thomasina is lying above, her ear pressed to the floor-boards.'

'No, I'm not, Irishman!' the maid's voice echoed down the dark passageway. 'I know your sort. I'm here with the biggest broom I can lay my hands on!'

Both Kathryn and Colum laughed. The Irishman sketched a bow and walked to the kitchen door.

'Oh.' He paused and spun round. 'I also bring messages from your friends, Alderman Newington and Master Luberon. They have studied the names of the doctors and apothecaries in Canterbury and have drawn up a list of those they think could be suspects. We are to meet them tomorrow in the Guildhall at eleven o'clock. Good night, Mistress Swinbrooke. My thanks for your hospitality.'

Kathryn smiled over her shoulder. 'Good night to you, Master Murtagh, and may the angels speed you to your rest.'

Kathryn's joke was not lost on Colum as a very thick-set "angel" in the person of Thomasina, who looked even more fearsome in a long nightgown buttoned closely at the neck, escorted him to the door and, with a loud sniff, slammed it firmly shut behind him. Colum grinned and made his way carefully across the cobbles to a small tavern on the far corner, the Black Jack, where he had stabled his horse. A sleepy ostler trotted it out and Colum, patting and talking to it gently, led it out into the street. He was still thinking of the story he had told Mistress Swinbrooke whilst ideas and thoughts sparkled like lights in his mind, images from the past: his mother, red-haired and white-faced, leaning over him; an old harpist thrilling him with the exploits of Cuchulain; a darkened passageway in some cold sombre tower in Ireland; dark green glens whipped up by a bold cutting wind; strange crosses inscribed in a language now forgotten; the thunder of horses' hooves, the bloody swirl of battle and the sense of being lost, of having no family. Colum was about to mount his horse but stopped as a soft voice called out in Gaelic from the shadows.

'Colum Ma fiach! Colum my son! Do not turn round. I bear messages from your brothers in Ireland.'

The voice was gentle. Colum suspected it was an old man but sensed he was in no danger. The Hounds would have struck immediately.

'They sent you this message, Colum Ma fiach. Say to Colum we have not forgotten him, but as the Bible says, "There is a season under Heaven for everything: a time for peace and a time for killing." Remember that!'

Colum, one hand resting on the horn of his saddle, waited for a while before turning round, but when he peered into the shadows, no one was there. He felt the hairs on the nape of his neck curl, as if some cold hand had gently caressed him. He thought of the white-faced Dog Priest; the voice reminded Colum of him. Somewhere in the streets beyond a dog suddenly howled, baying at the moon. Colum mounted, cursing the demons which still haunted him.

Chapter 5

Kathryn rose early the next morning. Thomasina was already bustling around the kitchen. She had started the fire, washed the metal cups and sharp-looking knives and, in accordance with instructions given by Kathryn's father long ago, heated such implements over the fire. Kathryn, dressed in a long, tawny-coloured gown, stood and watched her. She forgot the reason her father had insisted on this; he had always recommended it after a journey to Oxford to study the writings in a precious manuscript kept in Duke Humphrey's library. Agnes, still drugged with sleep, wandered round the kitchen like a dream-walker. Thomasina shouted and even gently cuffed the girl on the arm before losing her temper and telling her to go and wash her hands and face in the butt of cold water out in the garden.

They breakfasted on bread and watered ale. Kathryn, lost in her own thoughts, remained impervious to Thomasina's sulks and grumblings about entertaining ragged-arsed soldiers. When Thomasina found such tactics did not work, she eventually confronted Kathryn as she stood in her writing-chamber getting herbal pots out of a cupboard built against the wall.

'Well, what do you think?' Thomasina snapped.

'Of what?'

'Kathryn, do not play games. What kind of man is Murtagh?'

Kathryn smiled. 'Of mankind,' she quipped.

'And that letter?' Thomasina added accusingly.

'Just someone's stupid malice.'

'What do such notes say? It's not the first!'

Kathryn closed her eyes. She had vowed not to brood over the malicious letters. They came from a person with a sick mind. Perhaps they would stop if she did not react.

'So,' Thomasina persisted defiantly. 'The Irishman?'

'A mere shadow. I hardly think of him.'

Thomasina let out a great sigh and flounced away.

'What do I really think of him?' Kathryn murmured to herself. She stared at the small earthenware jar, its top covered by a scrap of hardened parchment held in place by a piece of twine. 'Strange,' she answered her own question. 'I find him strange and dangerous.' She heard a knock at the door, the first patient of the morning.

She tied her hair more firmly back, readjusted her veil and slipped her feet into leather-thonged pattens. Her first patient, Beatrice, the daughter of Henry the sack-maker, was an augury of how difficult the day would be. Henry was a small man with popping eyes, his bald head covered in fluffs of hair. With his fat jowls and protuberant lips, he always reminded Kathryn of a rather large carp. His daughter Beatrice, gaunt, white-faced, dull of eye and slack of jaw, was just recovering from a fit she had suffered the previous evening.

'What can I do?' the little man wailed, pushing his poor daughter down on a stool in the kitchen.

Kathryn sat opposite and held the girl's hand.

'You shouldn't have brought her,' she murmured. Her eyes pleaded with Henry. 'There is little I can do.'

Henry shuffled from foot to foot. 'Venta, the wise

woman,' he retorted, 'says a hole should be opened into her skull to let the evil humours out.'

Kathryn tightened her lips. Venta was a grey-haired, evil-smelling old harridan. She lived in the slums to the north of the city and made a fortune peddling coloured water or making outrageous claims. Kathryn peered at Beatrice's eyes, noticing how the irises were enlarged. She took a piece of wool and dabbed at the spittle trickling from the corner of the girl's mouth.

'If you follow Venta's advice,' she whispered gently, 'the girl will die. I have seen it before.'

Henry pointed a finger at the blooding cups and small row of sharp knives lying on the table.

'Then why not bleed her?'

Kathryn stared into Beatrice's listless face.

'If I do that, I'll kill her.'

She went back to her small medical chamber, took two pieces of parchment and scraped a small portion of powder into each of these and returned to the kitchen.

'Mix both of these with watered wine.'

'What are they?' Henry asked.

'A mixture of patis flora and poppy seed.' Kathryn pressed them into the sack-maker's reluctant hand. 'I am sorry there is nothing else I can do,' she added. 'Except, as I have said before, when your daughter has one of these attacks, make sure she lies straight and that her tongue is free in her mouth. When she recovers give her good broth and a cup of full-bodied wine, and in the evening, this medicine mixed in watered wine.'

Henry's lower lip jutted out farther. Kathryn thought he was about to refuse.

'I am not God,' she murmured.

Thomasina came up behind them. 'You could pray,' the maid said gently.

'Where?' Henry snapped. 'At the shrine? We have heard the stories; there's a killer loose!'

The sack-maker threw his coins down on the table, and

with the medicine clutched in one hand and steering his daughter Beatrice with the other, he stomped out of the room.

Other patients arrived. Torquil the carpenter, who had cut his hand and neglected to wash it. Now the wound was full of greenish-yellow pus. Kathryn cleaned it with vinegar and wine, which made Torquil yelp. Thomasina told him off for being such a baby, then applied a mixture of dried milk containing powder ground from dried moss. Mollyns the miller came next, the beak of a magpie slung round his neck. He held the right side of his jaw and moaned constantly. His whey-faced wife, Alice, trailing behind him, gave a graphic description of his savage toothache.

'He can't sleep at night,' she wailed. 'And neither can I. He is like a dog with three legs. The corn hasn't been ground. He snaps at his customers and takes his staff to the apprentice.'

'Why the magpie beak?' Kathryn asked, pushing Mollyns down into the chair and asking Thomasina to bring a candle closer.

'I was always told it would cure the toothache,' Mollyns moaned.

Kathryn wrinkled her nose. 'It smells. Open your mouth, Mollyns my lad.'

The miller obeyed. Kathryn brought the candle close, making sure it didn't scorch Mollyn's tangle of beard and moustache. She stared into the cavernous mouth, trying not to show her distaste at the sour, fetid breath. Mollyn's teeth, surprisingly enough, were quite white and clean, except one at the back, which looked black and ugly, the gum around it red and inflamed. Kathryn handed the candle back to Thomasina.

'How do you keep your teeth so white and clean?' she asked.

'I'm not here for the bloody good ones!' the miller

snapped, his little piggy eyes glaring at Kathryn. 'Your father wouldn't have asked such a stupid question!'

'Shut up, Mollyns!' Thomasina jibed. 'I have known you since you were a lad. You always had a big mouth and an itchy hand. The toothache is God's judgement on you for using faulty weights and mixing dust with your flour.'

'No, he does not!' the miller's wife shouted back. 'And I know you, Thomasina!'

'Good, good,' Kathryn intervened. 'Then we all know each other. I asked your husband a simple question. Do you clean your teeth with salt and vinegar?'

'Never touch the stuff.'

'He likes apples,' Alice said, coming closer. 'He's always eating them. We've got a small orchard. He eats more than the pig does.'

Kathryn smiled her thanks and vowed to remember this. She had observed the same before with Falloton the fruiterer and Horkle the grocer. Had her father been right? He had been forever claiming that the monks of Christchurch had healthy teeth and gums because they ate more fruit than meat. Mollyns suddenly moaned and Kathryn stared down at his red, angry, wart-covered face.

'Mollyns,' she said. 'I can do nothing. The tooth must come out and you must go to a barber-surgeon. But look.' Kathryn opened the case of ointments Thomasina always put on the table. She took a piece of washed wool, rolled it into a small ball and soaked it in oil of cloves. She told Mollyns to open his mouth and pressed this on the aching tooth, making the miller yelp. She then handed a phial of the oil to the miller's wife.

'Until he goes to a barber-surgeon and gets it plucked out, do the same again at noon and before he retires.'

Kathryn suddenly wrinkled her nose. Alice looked at her guiltily.

'What is the matter, Mistress?'

Kathryn drew close and saw Thomasina's look of distaste.

'Alice, are you well?'

'Why?'

'What is that terrible smell?'

Alice looked fleetingly at her husband but he was lost in his own circle of pain as the oil of cloves seeped in and began to soothe the rottenness in his tooth. Alice touched her head.

'It hurts me,' she whispered.

Without waiting, Kathryn pushed back Alice's hood and noticed how the woman's grey hair was thickly coated with grease.

'What have you put on it?' Kathryn exclaimed.

'The pain started,' Alice moaned, 'when his tooth began to hurt. So I rubbed . . .'

Kathryn pushed her nose closer. 'Oh, no, Alice, not that!'

The miller's wife looked guiltily away.

'Goat's cheese!' Kathryn exclaimed. 'You rubbed goat's cheese into your head!' She hid her smile. 'Alice, come here.'

The miller's wife, now rather frightened, stepped closer.

'Have I done wrong?' she wailed.

'Of course you have,' Thomasina said, stepping away hurriedly.

'What will happen now?'

'Come,' Kathryn said gently, and, whilst the miller sat moaning on a stool, Kathryn turned the woman round and gingerly felt the back of her neck and shoulders. The muscles there were tight and rigid. Kathryn began to stroke them gently and Alice let out a sigh of relief.

'Oh, Mistress, that feels good.'

'The humours in your neck,' Kathryn explained, 'are tense and taut. You have children?'

Alice, turning her neck, smiled.

'Four boys and three girls,' she said proudly.

'And when they fall, what do you do?' Kathryn asked.

'I rub their knees.'

'We are no different,' Kathryn murmured. 'Rub your neck vigorously with your hand. Wash that filthy mess out of your hair. Take a deep cup of claret before you retire for bed. Make sure you rest your head properly against the bolster and the pains will go.'

Alice nodded and smiled, but the smile promptly faded when she looked at her husband. She grabbed him by the shoulder.

'Now you, good husband, will get that tooth removed before you send all our wits flying!' And Alice angrily hustled her moaning husband out of the house.

For the next hour Kathryn and Thomasina dealt with a stream of minor ailments—cuts, bruises and other complaints. Kathryn looked despairingly at the hour-candle on its iron spike outside the buttery. She was busier than she thought and could not possibly visit Father Cuthbert at the Poor Priests' Hospital. Colum Murtagh appeared again in her mind and she felt a flutter of trepidation in her stomach. Colum had, like some shadow, lingered in her thoughts all morning and she realised how changeable his nature was, a man of violence trying to live at peace. He had brought other dangers with him. One of her patients had already mentioned the killings in Canterbury, so the news was beginning to spread.

'What is it, Mistress?' Thomasina interrupted.

Kathryn shook herself from her reverie and realised she was just standing there holding a jar of ointment.

'Thomasina, the Irishman doesn't worry me, but the business at the Guildhall does.'

'Oh, they are just a group of fat men,' her maid joked back. 'The Archbishop, he's as crafty as a fox. Luberon's a pompous piece of work, and don't be taken in by Newington, all meek and mild like some milksop. I disagree with your father's judgement on him. Newington's a viper in the grass, with a nasty tongue and a mind to match.'

'No.' Kathryn shook her head. 'It's not that, Thomasina, it's the killer.' She sat down on a stool. 'You heard what Henry the sack-maker said this morning. People know about the deaths.'

'Well?'

'Don't you see, Thomasina, sooner or later the killer will get to know about me. Will he add a woman physician and an Irish soldier to his list of unfortunate victims?'

Thomasina laughed and shrugged, but Kathryn knew she too had perceived the danger.

'We have to go,' Kathryn murmured. 'We must be at the Guildhall by eleven o'clock.'

She took off the wooden pattens, putting on hose and a pair of boots under her dress, for the streets would be messy with offal and dirt. She collected her old woollen cloak and the notes she had made the previous day. She was about to leave when there was a harsh knock at the front door. Thomasina, breathing curses, hurried down and came back accompanied by a young, well-dressed woman. A pure woollen cloak round her shoulders hid a tawny cloth dress braided at the top with fine green embroidery work. Her hair was covered with a white veil of pure lawn, which emphasized precise but very pretty features, clear grey eyes, a small nose, and generous red lips. Kathryn guessed she was no more than seventeen or eighteen summers old.

'You are Kathryn Swinbrooke?'

The question was abrupt but Kathryn saw the girl was nervous, so she smiled and nodded. The woman peeled off leather gloves, displaying a silver wedding band on the ring finger of her left hand.

'I need to talk to you,' the girl stammered. 'My name is Mathilda, wife of Sir John Buckler.'

'Well, we're just leaving,' Thomasina interrupted.

The girl stared pleadingly at Kathryn, her clear eyes now brimming with tears. 'I need to see you,' she repeated. 'I need your help.'

Kathryn walked over and caught Mathilda by the hand, warm and smooth like the sheen of silk. She would have stayed, for the Bucklers were powerful in Canterbury and Kathryn intuitively knew the matter was something deeply intimate. Had the girl been foolish and become pregnant by another man? Hence the cloak swathed tightly around her body? Or was it something else?

'Mistress Buckler, I cannot see you now.'

The girl looked as if she was going to burst into tears.

'But if you could come back'—Kathryn stopped as she considered what the routine of a great household must be—'sometime this evening? Shall we say before the bells chime for Vespers? I can see you then.'

The young woman looked away, wetting her lips with the pink tip of her tongue. 'I can . . .' She nodded her head. 'Yes, yes, I will come then.' She turned and Thomasina escorted her from the house.

Kathryn shrugged and breathed a prayer. She did not like such visitors, secretive and sly. She was a physician, a herbalist, not some night-hag with her hot needles and potions ready to clean a woman's womb.

'Trouble there,' Thomasina observed, coming back.

'Let's wait and see,' Kathryn murmured.

Thomasina called Agnes, left her instructions and she and Kathryn departed for the Guildhall. Kathryn ignored Thomasina's apparent disappointment about not going to the Poor Priests' Hospital and led her through winding alley-ways towards Hethenman Lane. She did not want to be stopped or greeted, so when she saw Goldere strutting towards her like a pompous duck, she slipped down a side street, breathing a sigh of relief that he did not pursue her. The alley-way led into a small enclosure filled with battered market-stalls and thronged with pedlars, hucksters and all the mountebanks who flocked to Canterbury to fleece the pilgrims. A small stage had been set up and a young man, some tattered scholar, was trying to earn a penny or crust of bread by loud declamations of poetry which everyone ignored. He looked so pale and waif-like, Kathryn felt sorry and stopped to listen before dropping a penny into the man's dirt-grimed hand. The student stopped and grinned.

'Thank you, Mistress. Not everyone appreciates poor Chaucer and his tales.'

Kathryn smiled, walked on, then abruptly stopped.

'Oh, sweet Lord!' she murmured.

'Mistress?' Thomasina pushed her angry face towards Kathryn. 'Mistress, what's wrong?'

'The murderer,' Kathryn whispered. 'I now know . . .'

'What is it, Mistress?'

Kathryn stared up at the spires of Canterbury Cathedral. Of course, she thought, Chaucer and his tales, or, more appropriately, the Prologue of his great poem, which her father had loved and helped her memorise: Chaucer had written about pilgrims, the murderer struck at pilgrims; Chaucer had listed their professions, the assassin picked his victims by profession. The doggerel verses parodied Chaucer and the quotation 'Radix malorum . . .' wasn't that from one of Chaucer's tales?

'Mistress!'

'Nothing.' Kathryn murmured and she walked on, leaving a baffled Thomasina to trail behind her.

Kathryn, finding it hard to contain her excitement, moved down the High Street, where the crowds milled round the stalls and booths. At last she knew how the murderer selected his victims, and she felt a small glow of triumph. Suddenly there were cries of horror from the crowd and Thomasina was scrabbling on her arm. The clamour on the High Street had stilled and the people stood aside for a huge cart pulled by two great black horses with shabby scarlet plumes nodding between their ears. The driver was hooded and masked, the black cowl fitting snugly round his head, the red mask crudely cut with slits for mouth and eyes. Animal bones, strung on a piece of string, hung round the driver's neck. Beside him, a young boy, similarly garbed, beat out the death-march on a small tambour.

'Sweet Jesu, help us!' Thomasina breathed.

The executioner's cart pushed its way through, down to Westgate. As the cart passed Kathryn, its dirty canvas covering slipped aside and Kathryn felt her gorge rise at the decapitated heads, blood-spattered and gory, and the human quarters, pickled in brine salt, which lay there.

'Good Jesu, have mercy on them!' she exclaimed.

'They are taking them to the city gates,' someone near her murmured.

'Who were they?' Thomasina asked.

'Rebels,' Kathryn replied. 'Men who supported Lancaster in the recent war. Sheriffs, lords, officials.'

'They haven't caught Nicholas Faunte yet!' a stall owner shouted.

'What does it matter?' Thomasina snapped. 'The war is over, the victors always have their blood-letting, then it's life back to normal.'

The crowd's enthusiasm and the warm summer weather had been blighted by the executioner's passage. Even the wealthy in their costly gowns, with large fat purses swinging from embroidered belts, put their heads down and muttered nervously to each other. Kathryn pushed her way past them to the steps of the Guildhall. Soldiers wearing the livery of York stood there. She saw Colum waiting, talking earnestly to a serjeant dressed in the royal livery, a short, thick-set, balding man, who looked every inch the professional soldier. Colum turned, glimpsed Kathryn and waved her over.

'You are well, Mistress Swinbrooke?'

'As fine as the day,' Kathryn replied. She looked over her shoulder. 'That cart and its driver! It was like being passed by Death itself!'

'They were executed yesterday,' the soldier standing next to Colum said, 'in the market-place at Maidstone. But once Faunte is captured—and we know he's hiding in the weald of Kent . . .' The fellow turned and spat. 'Then it's all over for us soldiers. Apart from royal favourites, like the Irishman here.'

Colum grinned, his tense face relaxed. 'Mistress Swinbrooke, physician, may I introduce Master Holbech: a serjeant by training, of indeterminate parentage, by birth a Yorkshireman.'

The hard blue eyes of the soldier caught Kathryn's and he nodded slightly. 'Mistress, your servant.'

Kathryn half-smiled whilst behind her Thomasina coughed and muttered loudly, 'Another guest for the hangman!'

Holbech swayed slightly to one side, winked at Thomasina and ran his tongue round his lips.

'Stay where you are,' Thomasina muttered.

'Master Holbech,' Colum continued hurriedly, as if he sensed their animosity, 'is no longer in the royal service. I have hired him to help me at Kingsmead. He and a few other rogues whose war-waging days are over. Kingsmead is nothing more than a derelict building. We need carpenters, farriers, smiths and craftsmen, and Holbech is the man to pluck a rose from the Queen without her knowing it.'

Holbech shuffled his big boots at such praise just as a woman, thick red hair straggling behind her, ran across the street from St Helen's Church and caught Holbech by his arm. Amber, cat-like eyes stared from a pointed white face. The woman smiled at Colum, then coolly studied Kathryn, who just stared back. The woman's brown smock was ill-fitting, but it still emphasized the voluptuous curves of hip and breast whilst her red hair, massed round her white face, seemed like a fiery halo.

'This is Megan, Holbech's woman,' Colum said flatly. Colum clasped the serjeant's hand. 'Well, Holbech, you have your orders and I have mine.' He tapped the thick heavy wallet which swung from the soldier's sword-belt. 'You have silver and warrants enough. Buy what you have to, hire whom you need. The work has to be done within a month. The King will soon disband his army and the horses will be sent south.'

Holbech nodded at Kathryn and moved away. Megan still clung to his arm, chattering like a child whilst looking provocatively over her shoulder at Colum.

The Irishman watched them go.

'A good man,' he murmured. 'A bit of a bastard.' He ignored the sharp hiss of disapproval from Thomasina. 'But she's trouble.' He turned and walked up the Guildhall steps, hardly waiting for Kathryn to join him.

'How do you know?' Thomasina impishly asked.

Colum stopped and turned. 'How do I know what?'

'That Megan's trouble?'

'Holbech and I have fought the length and breadth of the kingdom. Megan's a camp follower, a good woman, she looks after her man. The problem is that she moves from one to another like a butterfly flits from flower to flower. She stirs up trouble, as Holbech will soon find out.'

Colum strode into the Guildhall. Kathryn pulled a face at Thomasina behind his back and followed suit. The entrance-way was thronged with royal messengers and officials both from the court and city. The atmosphere was a mixture of dread and excitement as these soldiers and officials, Colum included, searched records, hunted down traitors and brought the city of Canterbury back under royal rule. An officious tipstaff approached them. Colum mentioned Newington and Luberon and the fellow led them off down a passageway past chambers, their doors half-open, where clerks sat on high stools transcribing letters or documents.

Newington and Luberon were waiting for them in the main hall. They were sitting behind a table, whilst in front of them, seated on stools, were five individuals, their backs to the door. As soon as he glimpsed Kathryn and Colum, Newington rose, his thin pallid face breaking into a false smile. He appeared more calm and collected than the previous day. His hair was coiffured, his thin beard and moustache neatly clipped, and he wore a scarlet gown trimmed with squirrel fur, with the gold chain of office round his neck. Luberon looked pompous and ink-stained as ever, but he scurried forward to meet them, bobbing like a leaf in a water butt.

'Master Murtagh, Mistress Swinbrooke, you are most welcome.'

He ushered them towards a desk as the others rose and turned to meet them. Kathryn kept her eyes down as Luberon brought up chairs for her and Colum.

The introductions were made. Kathryn was described as Mistress Swinbrooke, physician. She heard a snort of laughter and looked up, fighting back the rush of anger. The five men were all strangers, except for Geoffrey Cotterell. The latter stood there, oil-soaked strands of hair carefully combed across his balding head, his protuberant fish-like eyes and slobbery lips sneering at her, his thumbs poked in the expansive girdle round his barrel-like waist. He flicked dust from his fur-trimmed gown and grinned maliciously at Kathryn. Cotterell had hated Kathryn's father and had little patience for his daughter with her so-called airs, graces and titles. Kathryn ignored his sneer and sat down. Colum, next to her, eased his long legs out, crossing his ankles. He looked warningly at Cotterell and wiped the sneer from the physician's face. Newington continued the introductions. Kathryn did not recognise any of the rest, though she had heard of their names and reputations as leading physicians in Canterbury. James Brantam, young and nervous, with reddish hair and protuberant front teeth, crouched like a nervous rabbit, wetting his lips and looking sideways at Cotterell. Kathryn knew that Brantam owned a shop and practice near Westgate. Matthew Darryl, dark, with deep-set eyes, was a smooth-shaven, pleasant-faced young man. Newington coughed when he introduced him and explained that

Darryl was his son-in-law. Next to him, tall and angular, sharp-featured, with a rather wispy moustache and a beak-like nose, was Edmund Straunge. And finally there was Roger Chaddedon. Tall, dark and graceful, with smooth olive skin and clear eyes, he wore his costly physician's gown above the cream cambric shirt with a grace and poise denied to the others. Chaddedon caught Kathryn's eye and smiled. She looked away in embarrassment. Chaddedon was handsome and she recalled his reputation as a good doctor who charged fair fees and treated the poor free. Kathryn's father had often praised him and she felt a pang of sadness that they had not known him when her father was alive. He would have liked Chaddedon. Indeed, his calm manner and friendly approach reminded Kathryn of her father.

Nevertheless, all the doctors seemed a little uneasy at why they had been summoned, and Newington's introduction of Colum as the King's Special Commissioner affected even Chaddedon's cool demeanour.

'So why are we here?' Cotterell asked sharply.

'You are all doctors, physicians,' Luberon piped up.

'So?' Straunge snapped. 'That is no crime!'

'You all own,' Luberon continued officiously, 'houses and shops in Canterbury and have access to potions and poisons denied to others.'

The group caught the drift of his words and shifted nervously on their stools. Luberon jabbed an ink-stained finger at Cotterell and Brantam.

'You two practise your skills independently. Cotterell near the Buttermarket, Brantam in Westgate. Whilst you three'—he waved a hand airily at Darryl, Straunge and Chaddedon—'have set up some sort of commune.'

Straunge quietly intervened. 'A collegium.'

'Ah, yes.' Luberon smiled falsely. 'A collegium near the city wall next to Queningate.'

'There's no crime in that,' Darryl murmured, his dark eyes watchful. 'What are you implying? In London it is common practice for doctors to share their skills and pool their monies.' He laughed nervously and pointed to his father-in-law, Newington. 'Even our good alderman has some share in our profits.'

Chaddedon leaned forward. 'Master Luberon, Alderman Newington and'—he glanced sharply at Colum and Kathryn—'your companions.'

Thomasina was ignored. She sat at the far end of the room on a window-seat, idly staring out through the panes of glass, though Kathryn knew she was listening to every word.

'Master Luberon,' Chaddedon continued, 'you have described our affairs, there is no crime in that. Unlike others in the city or on the council, we did not espouse the Lancastrian cause in the recent war, so why are we here?'

Colum abruptly stood up and went to the edge of the table, tapping noisily on it with his fist, and for the first time Kathryn glimpsed the strange Celtic rings on his fingers. She was sure he had not worn those the previous evening. The Irishman rapped the table-top again.

'You are all here,' he declared, 'to be questioned.'

'About what?' the physicians chorused.

Colum tapped the table-top again. 'About murder and sacrilege, crimes as sordid as any treason!'

Chapter 6

It took a great deal of table-rapping and shouting to subdue the clamour which broke out. Darryl and Straunge sprang to their feet, shouting and yelling at Luberon and Newington. Cotterell sat back open-mouthed, eyes staring, though Brantam looked a little relieved and Kathryn glimpsed the half-smile on his face. She watched the Irishman, however: he was a different man from her guest of the previous evening, utterly devoid of any gentleness or good humour, as if he resented these soft, wealthy men and was pleased to bring them to book. Chaddedon made to rise, gathering his cloak about him as if preparing to leave.

'Don't go!' Colum threatened. 'If you go out of that door, Sir, I shall arrest you for treason! Now'—he raised his voice to a shout—'all of you will sit down!'

Colum kept banging the top of the table until all the physicians had resumed their seats. Kathryn winced at the clattering noise. Colum glared at her, then at a puce-faced Luberon. Newington, however, just sat staring serenely into the middle distance, as if embarrassed by the fracas.

'There have been four murders here,' Colum began.

'Five,' Luberon interrupted.

'You did not tell me!' Colum accused.

'I had not time!' the clerk snapped. 'Yesterday afternoon a merchant, Philip Spurrier, was poisoned in the cathedral itself.' The clerk leaned his elbows on the table, steepling his fingers, enjoying the power and consternation caused by his announcement. 'The King's Commissioner,' he continued smoothly, 'Master Murtagh, now knows that five pilgrims. Five,' he repeated, 'have been poisoned whilst visiting the shrine of Saint Thomas à Becket.' He stilled the gasps and cries with his hand.

'Let us not act the innocent,' he mocked. 'You have heard the rumours and now you shall know it all. This assassin, this limb of Satan, knows Canterbury well. He has an easy supply of potions and poisons and actually announces who his next victim will be by pinning up doggerel verses on the cathedral door.' Luberon quickly went through the names and professions of the first four murders.

'The fifth?' Colum interrupted.

'Early yesterday afternoon,' Luberon answered. 'A lay brother brought this to us.' He picked up a greasy piece of parchment from the desk, and read:

'A merchant to Becket's shrine did go.
And I to Hell his soul did show.

'The merchant Spurrier was part of a group who visited the sacred shrine yesterday. They were later taken to the sacristry for refreshment. Spurrier drained his cup, and a few minutes later fell dead at the feet of his comrades.'

'And the murderer went unnoticed?' Kathryn's quiet voice stilled the clamour.

They all looked at her, rather surprised.

'Of course!' Luberon exclaimed. 'No one saw anything amiss. Oh, yes, the merchants did notice a stranger who joined their group, hooded and cowled, but they did not object. They thought he was another visitor who had paid a special fee. By the time Spurrier took his first sip from the cup, this man had gone.'

'And the body lies where?' Kathryn asked.

'In the death house at Saint Augustine's. The infirmarian claims Spurrier was killed by a strong infusion of hemlock.'

'A costly poison,' Straunge murmured.

'And these merchants?' Colum enquired.

'The merchants are at the Chequers Inn in Mercery Street,' Newington replied, smoothing his hands together. 'But, Master Luberon, we are not the coroner's court; the corpse does not concern us.'

'No, we are not.' Colum seized the initiative. 'But His Majesty the King and the Lord Archbishop have ordered me, Special Commissioner in Canterbury, to investigate, track down and hang this murderer before he desecrates one of the greatest shrines of Christendom.'

'And so, why us?' Straunge asked.

Colum smiled. 'There is no doubt that our murderer is an educated man, even though he scrawls doggerel verse. He knows the city of Canterbury and can flit like a shadow through the alley-ways and lanes and no one sees him. And he is someone with a deep-set grudge or grievance against the shrine, hence the murders. But most important, he is a doctor or a physician.' He tapped the table to still the shouts of protest. 'Only a doctor, a physician, someone with jars full of deadly potions and poisonous herbs could perpetrate these murders.'

Brantam leaned forward and tapped the table as if mimicking Colum.

'Master Commissioner, Lord of the Isles, or whatever you wish to call yourself. We are loyal subjects of the King, men of standing in our community. Are we suspect before the law? And if we are, why is this matter not being investigated by the sheriff or the coroner or'—Brantam looked accusingly at Newington—'the Council of Aldermen?'

'Because,' Newington replied, 'we have no sheriff, no mayor, no coroner, no Council of Aldermen! Thanks to Faunte and others of his ilk, the liberties of this city have been suspended. Master Murtagh acts for the King in this matter.'

'Come, come,' Luberon added tactfully.

Kathryn sensed the shift in mood. Previously Newington had appeared as the tactful, withdrawn one, but the little clerk had begun to impress her with his mastery of purpose and sharp reminders.

'Look, gentlemen.' Luberon pointed to the list on the table. 'I agree that in Canterbury there are other physicians and herbalists.' He spread his hands. 'Well, we have had to draw lines through many names on our list: those who are sick; those who are too old; those who do not have the means; those, like our good sister here, Mistress Kathryn Swinbrooke, who do not fit the description of the man we are hunting. Also, the sweating sickness has dealt a savage blow to your numbers. Thus, so far, you are the only ones who can be included in our list of suspects.'

'What about our good sister, Mistress Swinbrooke?' Darryl scoffed. 'She's a physician and an apothecary.' He smiled sourly. 'Well, that is, until her husband returns.'

'Mistress Swinbrooke,' Luberon asked gently. 'Would you like to answer your colleagues?'

'I need not,' Kathryn replied. 'But I will. Master Darryl, my father was a physician; he is dead, God rest him. My husband has gone to the wars, and God knows where he lays his head now. My father trained me and I have letters of licence from the Corporation. May I remind you, Master Darryl, that there is, as yet, no Guild of doctors or apothecaries in Canterbury, and I have the liberty to do as I think fit. Finally, like other brothers and sisters in our profession, I hold a key to the postern gates of the city, so I can leave and enter as I so wish to tend the sick and care for those patients beyond the city wall. To put it bluntly, Master Darryl, I am as good a physician as you are, but I am also a woman and therefore not on the list of suspects.' She rested her elbows on the high-backed chair and leaned forward. 'The Corporation, the King's Commissioner, and His Grace the Archbishop have hired me to help in this matter. I am no more pleased than you are about a killer stalking the streets of Canterbury and murdering pilgrims according to their occupation.'

Kathryn paused and licked her lips. She felt surprised at her own anger. These men were not like her father. He had been so gentle; they were arrogant and patronising. She glanced sideways at Colum. He was chewing the corner of his mouth in an attempt to hide a grin. I'll settle with you later, Irishman, she thought and fleetingly wondered if she should announce how she had discovered the method the murderer used to select his victims. However, Newington and Luberon were becoming distracted and beginning to sift amongst their papers.

'I have no doubt,' she concluded quietly, 'that this murderer is a burgess of Canterbury and a physician. Who else has access to poisons and knows how to dilute them in wine? If any lay person bought these, it would arouse suspicion. And they are costly, even more so now, for the trade has been hampered by the recent war.'

She was pleased to see Chaddedon, even Straunge and Darryl, nod solemnly at her words.

'The Corporation, the King,' Luberon added quickly, 'have drawn an indenture up with Mistress Swinbrooke.' He smiled fleetingly at her. 'Which will be given to her later.' He spread his hands. 'So, gentlemen, you now know as much as we do for your presence here.'

'But anyone,' Straunge interrupted heatedly, 'anyone with a good herb garden could concoct such fusions. Even you, Master Luberon. Are you not a lover of flowers? Indeed, the Archbishop himself, so I understand, has entrusted his rose garden to you. You are also a herbalist, well-known for your enquiries amongst the apothecaries and physicians of the city.'

Luberon's mouth opened and closed as Straunge's remark struck home. Colum moved restlessly and Kathryn felt a prickle of fear at the nape of her neck. Straunge was right. The murderer might still be anyone with a knowledge of herbs and physic, but then she remembered the foxglove mixed in the dead doctor's white wine.

'Master Straunge, you may be correct,' she spoke up. 'A child can collect foxglove or deadly fungi, but to grind them to make the powders, to know the measure and how to mix them? You must agree that requires great skill.'

The tension drained from Luberon's face. Straunge shrugged and smiled.

'Concedo,' he said. 'Master Luberon, I meant no offence. I was simply making a point.'

'You, we,' Kathryn spoke up swiftly, 'could all be innocent. I am sure,' she lied, 'you all are. Nevertheless . . .'

'Nevertheless,' Colum interrupted harshly, 'you must answer certain questions. We have little evidence about the other murder victims except how they died. Master Cotterell, I believe you tended one?'

The pompous physician, who had now lost his arrogance, nodded quickly. 'I was simply nearby,' he squeaked.

'We shall leave that death for now,' Colum continued. 'But I will question you all about your movements and business yesterday afternoon, when Spurrier was poisoned in the cathedral. I am the King's Commissioner and, on your allegiance, you must answer truthfully. Mistress Swinbrooke, with her knowledge of physic, will assist.'

Suddenly Brantam rose nervously to his feet.

'Sit down!' Colum ordered.

'I need to speak to Mistress Swinbrooke,' Brantam stuttered. 'But privately.' The anxiety in his face was apparent for all to see and his hands kept clutching his costly coat with its lining of dyed lamb's-wool. 'Please! Please!' he begged. 'Mistress Swinbrooke?'

Before Colum could intervene, Kathryn stood up.

'Does this have any bearing on this matter?' she asked.

Brantam nodded.

'Gentlemen, you will excuse us?'

She led Brantam out of the room; Thomasina made to rise, but Kathryn gestured at her to remain.

Outside in the passageway, Brantam walked up and down.

'What is it, Sir?' Kathryn asked.

Brantam just shook his head, then opened and shut his mouth. Kathryn ignored him for a while, distracted by a fierce discussion farther down the passageway. A group of swan-uppers in their dirty jerkins, leather breeches and mud-encrusted boots were shouting at an official about payment for looking after the royal swans on the river Stour.

'Master Brantam, shall we return?' Kathryn asked.

The young man shook his head. 'I can prove,' he began, 'I can prove that until two days ago I had been out of the city for ten days. I journeyed up to London.'

'But you were in Canterbury yesterday when Spurrier died?'

'Yes, yes, I was.'

'So?'

'I was in Canterbury, so to speak, but yesterday, from noon until the burghmote, well . . . until the burghmote horn sounded in the market to end the day's business'—Brantam licked his lips—'I was in Master Cotterell's house.'

'And he was with you?'

'No, I was with his wife in their bedchamber.'

Kathryn tightened her lips to hide her smile. Now she could see why Brantam had been so nervous. The young physician looked pleadingly at her.

'Can't you see, Mistress? I have proof where I was, but if Cotterell finds out, he might kill both her and me!'

'What proof do you have?'

Brantam looked shamefacedly away.

'If you go to the Cotterell house'—he looked fleetingly up at Kathryn—'and I know you might; in the bedchamber, the bolsters are made of red silk with two white turtle-doves entwined in a circle of blue Canterbury bells. Mistress Cotterell, her stockings were red, yellow-clocked. Ask her! She has a mole on her right thigh near . . .' Again Brantam wetted his lips. 'Near her secret parts.'

Kathryn now had her lower lip firmly between her teeth. She felt sorry for the man but couldn't ignore the humour of the situation.

'I swear this. I'm always there, whenever I have the chance. I love her!'

The door suddenly swung open and Colum came out.

'Mistress Swinbrooke, what is the matter?'

'Go home, Master Brantam,' Kathryn said quietly.

Colum shouldered past her. 'Sir, you will not!'

Brantam's eyes beseeched Kathryn.

'Master Brantam,' she repeated, 'you will go home, and if this gentleman stops you, I will go with you. Go on!'

Brantam turned and almost ran down the corridor. Colum seized Kathryn by the arm, his dark face a mask of fury. She hid her fear at the chilling look in his eyes. His lips were tight in a snarl and she could see the muscle flicker high in his cheek.

'I will say,' he grated, 'who comes and who goes!'

'Irishman, let go of my arm!'

'I will!'

'Sir, let go of my arm, you're hurting me!' Kathryn stepped closer. Colum's hand fell away. Kathryn rubbed where his vise-like grip had made her muscle ache. 'I'll have a bruise there,' she said. 'For God's sake, man, Brantam's no murderer. An adulterer, yes, in Master Cotterell's bed!'

Colum's face changed. The anger disappeared and he looked tired, blinking furiously, as if disassociating himself from the fury of a few seconds earlier.

'By the rood!' he muttered. 'Come back, Kathryn. I'm sorry!'

They rejoined the rest of the group, Colum shamedfacedly declaring that Mistress Swinbrooke had information which prevented further questioning of Master Brantam. He then asked a few more questions, establishing that the rest of the physicians had been in Canterbury when Spurrier's murder had taken place. Finally Colum nodded at Newington, who stood up and gestured for silence.

'This matter will be kept secret,' the alderman declared. 'It has begun without any grace or favour, even my own son-in-law, married to my beloved daughter Marisa, is under suspicion. Indeed, we all are, for these murders threaten the shrine, the pilgrims and the trade of a city already labouring under its false allegiance to the House of Lancaster. The King's Commissioner and Mistress Swinbrooke will undoubtedly question each of you.' Newington wiped his sweat-soaked hands on the front of his robe. 'You are not to leave the city but continue on your own affairs.' He beamed around. 'That not only includes the skill of physic but all other matters.' He smiled down the table at Kathryn and Colum. 'My son-in-law, indeed, all the others here, are Masters of the Guild of Jesus's Mass. We are preparing the Corpus Christi play at Holy Cross Church in Westgate. When it is ready and these matters are finished, you must join us there.'

'I will question you all,' Colum repeated, ignoring Newington's pleasantries. 'But for the moment, Sirs, you are all dismissed.'

The physicians rose and hurriedly left, though Chaddedon lingered to smile and sketch a courteous bow at Kathryn.

'Mistress Swinbrooke,' he offered, 'for my part, you will always be a most welcome guest in our house.'

Kathryn smiled, choosing to ignore Colum's furious glare at the physician's retreating back.

Once the door had closed behind them, Luberon went to a table in the corner and poured out five goblets of wine, serving Newington, Kathryn, Colum and finally Thomasina. For a while, after such a heated debate, they just sat reflecting on what they had learnt. Luberon asked about Brantam but Colum smiled and murmured how the young doctor had worries of his own.

'What happens now?' Kathryn asked, rising to ease the cramp in her legs. She felt slightly elated. For the first time since the death of her father she was no longer floating like some leaf on a stream but responsible for what was happening around her. Luberon smiled and Kathryn glimpsed the genuine humour in the little clerk's eyes.

'You enjoyed that, Mistress Swinbrooke, interrogating your colleagues?'

Kathryn grinned mischievously, her eyes twinkling. 'I did not know you were such a keen gardener, Master Clerk.'

Luberon coughed. 'I am, after a fashion, and Straunge is correct, I have an interest in herbs. But I am not a killer, and yesterday I was working in the Archbishop's chancery.' He shook his head. 'I wondered if they would pounce on me.'

'Oh,' Kathryn quipped, 'whenever you put two or three physicians together, you always get into a dispute. But, Master Murtagh, what now?'

Colum sat slumped in his chair, lost in his own thoughts.

'I have asked the merchants,' Newington intervened, squinting at the hour-candle winking on its spigot at the corner of the room, 'those who were with Spurrier when he died, to join us. They'll arrive at the second hour, but, Master Murtagh, remember you have other business?'

Colum drummed his fingers on the arms of his chair. 'I know, I know, petty disputes. They do not concern me.'

'You are the King's Commissioner,' Newington continued smoothly. 'You work in the marshalsea of the royal household, and in the circumstances, these matters must be adjudicated by you.'

Colum made a rude sound with his lips and stared at Kathryn. He saw the flush of excitement high in her cheeks, and if he had had the courage, he would have complimented her on how lovely she was. Strange, he thought, Kathryn could change so quickly. She had struck him as comely, serene and rather withdrawn, but the heated debate with the physicians had sparked something in her and brought a passion to life. Colum looked guiltily away as Kathryn rose.

'I do have some information,' Kathryn announced, crossing to the door to make sure it was firmly closed. She walked into the centre of the room. 'I think,' she began falteringly, 'I think I know how the murderer selects his victims.'

The rest stared at her.

'You have heard,' Kathryn continued more firmly, 'of the poet Geoffrey Chaucer?'

Luberon smiled and nodded. Colum looked askance whilst Newington just shrugged his shoulders.

'Chaucer was a poet,' Kathryn continued, 'who lived, oh, about a hundred years ago during the reign of Richard the Second. My father was fond of quoting him.'

'Ah, yes,' Newington said. 'I have heard the name. He wrote a famous poem about Canterbury.'

'The Canterbury Tales,' Kathryn agreed. 'They include a prologue, a list of characters, a knight, a nun, a prior, a monk, a summoner. Indeed, virtually every occupation in society. They leave the Tabard Inn in Southwark one April morning to go to Becket's shrine. On the journey, as is the custom, they each tell a story.'

Colum still looked puzzled.

'Look,' Kathryn explained, 'my father often quoted the poet's verses. They were written in rhyming couplets very similar to the ones our murderer has left on the cathedral door.' She sighed and flailed her hands against her side. 'Can't you see? Our assassin's an educated man. He's read Chaucer's *Canterbury Tales.* His doggerel verse parodies that of Chaucer, and all the people he has murdered have identical occupations to the characters in Chaucer's prologue.'

'Too far-fetched,' Newington said.

'No, it isn't,' Luberon spoke up. 'Mistress Swinbrooke is correct. One of Chaucer's tags reads "Radix malorum est Cupiditas"—The love of money is the root of all evil. Don't you remember the assassin's verse:

'Becket's tomb all dirt and crass,
Radix malorum est Cupiditas.'

Luberon preened himself. 'I believe it's a quotation from "The Pardoner's Tale".'

Luberon then stood up and almost did a dance, his little feet shuffling, his pompous face wreathed in a smile. He clapped his hands like a child.

'Oh, very good, Mistress Swinbrooke!' he chortled. 'Very good indeed!'

'What use is it?' Colum asked peevishly. 'How many characters are in this Chaucer's *Tales?*'

Kathryn made a face. 'Oh, about twenty to thirty.'

'So what do we do?' Newington sneered. 'Find a copy of these tales and ban all such professions from Canterbury? Impossible! We are here to hang a murderer, not hunt for books.'

Luberon glared at him. 'No, no, there will be a copy in the cathedral library. The Cardinal Archbishop must own one.' He picked up his cloak and rearranged it on the back of the chair. 'When we are finished here, we must go there, Mistress Swinbrooke. All of us, and look at this book.'

Colum relaxed and winked at Kathryn.

'Mistress Swinbrooke, accept our congratulations. I do not wish to appear churlish; you may well have established one strand in our sorry tale. So we are looking for a murderer with a grievance against the shrine, who has read and studied this poet Chaucer. He may even possess a copy of his work? Master Luberon will take us to see this book?'

'Well, we can't go now,' Newington interrupted. He pointed to the hour-candle, where the winking flame had reached the ring marking the second hour. 'Let's finish our business here,' he grumbled. 'Mistress Kathryn, you need not stay, though this should not take long.'

He had hardly finished speaking when a tipstaff dressed in the city livery and carrying a silver-topped staff entered the room. He bent over the table and whispered to Colum and Luberon. The Irishman shrugged. Luberon cleared the papers from the table and gestured at Newington to join them. Kathryn went to join Thomasina, who sat in the window-seat pretending to doze.

'A great deal of chatter,' Thomasina murmured. 'If men were as good with their promises as they are with their mouths, the world would be a happier place.' She smiled and nudged Kathryn gently. 'You held your own well there,' she whispered. 'Look at Luberon! He's taken a liking to you! The Irishman's still a closed book whilst Master Chaddedon . . .' Thomasina drew back mockingly. 'A conquest there, yes, Mistress?'

'Be still!' hissed Kathryn, trying to hide her embarrassment and silence her loud-mouthed maid.

'If I was taking a wager,' Thomasina continued blithely, 'I would say you have met your murderer.' She nudged Kathryn again. 'Look at Alderman John Newington, he's a morose bastard!'

Kathryn looked across the table, where Luberon and Newington now sat on either side of Colum.

'He's always been miserable,' Thomasina said. 'He's not Canterbury-born, you know. He came here as a young man and built himself up as a cloth merchant. Very little family. His wife died years ago, but he has a married daughter.'

Thomasina drew in her breath to continue her report when the door was flung open and the tipstaff reentered. He banged his staff noisily on the floor, and Thomasina cursed.

'Silence!' the official shouted. 'So those who have business before the King's Commissioner may draw near and have their petitions redressed!'

'Oh, shut up, you pompous peacock!' Thomasina hissed in a loud whisper.

The tipstaff glared at her, banged his staff noisily again and a group of men entered the room. Kathryn must have sat for an hour watching Murtagh, the King's Commissioner in Canterbury, deal with petty civic affairs. The Bowyers' Guild had sent representatives claiming that bow staffs should be three inches thick, squared, and seven feet long, the wood to be well polished and without knots. They loudly protested how others were selling inferior, cheaper staffs. Colum quietly heard them out and ordered the market beadles to make a search. A dispute between the Guild of Black Bread Bakers and the Guild of White Bread Bakers was summarily dismissed. Avery Sabine was fined for keeping hogs in the churchyard; Goodman Trench for driving posts into the King's highway; Thomas Court for selling watery beer in wooden pots; Potterman, a barber-surgeon of St Peter's, was fined twopence for shaving a man on Sunday. Other petty cases followed, most of them settled in a few minutes. Kathryn admired Murtagh's cool detachment and the professional manner in which he dealt with these matters.

He's an actor, Kathryn thought, whether riding a horse,

hearing a case, administering the stables. What he does, he does well. But when his mask slips, what sort of man lies beneath? She watched the flame on the hour-candle move from the second to the third ring. At last Luberon announced the Court of Petty Sessions was over. Newington, crouching beside Colum, whispering advice on civic matters, agreed. The tipstaff went down the passageway and noisily informed the other plaintiffs to return another day.

'What now?' Thomasina moaned. She moved her large bottom on the window-seat.

'Don't wait,' Kathryn replied. 'This is taking longer than I thought. Go to the Rushmarket near Ridinggate. Buy fresh sheaves for the kitchen and I'll meet you at home.'

Thomasina gratefully stumped out whilst Colum waved Kathryn back to the table.

'You found that fascinating, Mistress Swinbrooke?'

'Not quite as much as you did.'

Colum shrugged. 'Between battles and horses, such was my task: Which member of the royal household could claim privilege? Who had been helping themselves in the pantry? Which of the royal scullions had cut meat from the spits?' Colum smiled and stretched. 'You English have a passion for the law.'

He was about to continue when the door was again flung open and the tipstaff led in a group of merchants. They were portly, well-dressed in their beaver hats, quilted doublets, costly hose and expensive leather boots, but they clung together like a group of frightened children, appalled by the sudden murder of their colleague. They all had one desire: to leave Canterbury as quickly as possible. Colum questioned them gently, but it was like trying to draw blood from a stone. The merchants knew of no one in Canterbury who had a grievance against the dead Spurrier. They had seen or heard nothing untoward.

'Oh, yes,' one of them confessed. 'We saw the stranger,

but we thought he was a monk; he was hooded and cowled, and then he disappeared.'

The rest of the group chorused agreement. Colum asked a few further questions, then courteously dismissed them. Once the merchants were gone, Kathryn, who had remained silent throughout the interrogation, stood and collected her cloak.

'There's nothing more we can do here.' She sighed. 'Master Luberon, the Chaucer manuscript?'

'I must go too,' Newington put in. He smiled sheepishly. 'I have to make my peace with my son-in-law and daughter. There's really no point in disturbing his Grace the Archbishop.' He tapped the small clerk on the shoulder. 'Luberon, you know more of libraries than I do. Ask his Grace the Cardinal if he has a copy of Chaucer's poem and have it sent to Mistress Swinbrooke's house in Ottemelle Lane.'

The clerk agreed, hurriedly collected his papers, quill and inkpot, put them in a leather bag and followed Newington out of the chamber. Kathryn and Murtagh left a few minutes later. As they walked down the sun-lit steps of the Guildhall, they had to shield their eyes against the bright glare of the afternoon sun. Colum patted his stomach.

'I am hungry, Mistress Swinbrooke. A bite to eat? Let me be your host.'

'I thought you didn't like taverns?'

'Mistress Swinbrooke, my throat is dry and my belly empty. If Thomasina was here, I'd eat her!'

Kathryn smiled and led him down into the High Street, now thronged with townspeople moving amongst the stalls. At the bottom of the Guildhall steps a man had been placed in a pillory, his ears pinned to the wooden slats on either side with a scrawled notice round his neck proclaiming that he had spoken contumaciously against the King. A group of nuns dressed in the black garb of the Order of the Holy Sepulchre were ministering to him, wiping the blood and sweat from his face and trying to make him sip from the cup of wine they held to the injured man's bloodied lips. Kathryn looked away.

'I wish people would keep a still tongue in their heads,' she murmured.

Colum guided her by the elbow through the busy market.

'Aye, Mistress, as they say in Ireland, many a man's tongue has cost him his head!'

They stood aside to let a funeral procession pass, the coffin bobbing on the shoulders of the drunken pallbearers. Four men carrying lighted tapers on either side were just as deep in their cups, so it looked more of a mummer's play than a funeral cortège.

'In the midst of life we are in death,' Kathryn observed.

'Live life to the full and see the days,' Colum retorted. 'Mistress Swinbrooke, I have visited the cathedral on many an occasion, but the city I don't really know. A good tavern?'

'The Lion in the Mercery,' Kathryn replied and moved to the right, past the Chequers Tavern, called the "Inn of a Hundred Beds," where pilgrims thronged in the wide portico. Some were preparing to leave the city, the metal badge depicting the head of St Thomas à Becket fastened to their coats or hats. Others had just arrived, pushing through the gateway into the yard, shouting for ostlers and gazing about in wide-eyed wonderment.

'If they only knew,' Kathryn whispered.

Suddenly, from the inn-yard, an Irish voice shouted, the words indistinct. Colum whirled round, his hand going to his knife, the other wrapping his thick woollen cloak shield, or buckler, round his arm. Kathryn gazed in amazement. Colum was no longer the graceful, sauntering Irishman but a fighter ready to strike and kill. He ignored Kathryn completely and gazed stony-eyed into the crowds thronging the great yard of the Chequers Tavern, as if expecting some enemy to attack.

Kathryn moved towards him but Colum drew his knife and pushed her gently aside.

'For God's sake, man!' Kathryn said.

Colum blinked and looked at her. 'You heard it!' he snapped. 'The Irish voice!'

'Of course, and there are Welsh, French, Bretons, visitors from Calais. Colum, what is the matter?'

At the tavern gate others were now looking towards the wild-eyed Irishman with his knife drawn. Kathryn heard the Irish voice calling, a man demanding service and cursing the ostler. Colum relaxed and resheathed his dagger. Kathryn took him gently by the wrist.

'Colum, you are fine?'

Colum grinned weakly.

'Aye, woman, nothing but ghosts from my past.'

Chapter 7

Kathryn and Colum moved farther down the Mercery, where the houses of the rich and poor stood cheek by jowl. The cottages of the artisans were nothing more than wooden huts with roofs of straw or rushes, low squat buildings with overhanging roofs which continually dripped water. The mansions of the rich, however, were built of stout beams and plaster, their roofs supported by columns formed into grotesque figures of goblins or grinning monsters and covered with knots, scrolls and other bizarre designs. Colum stared up at the narrow wedge of blue sky between the houses.

'I have never liked the city,' he muttered. He was still restless and kept his hand on his dagger. He peered down the narrow gloomy lanes which ran off the Mercery, so dark that, even during the day, lantern-horns had been lit and placed on hooks outside the doors. At last they entered the Lion. The taproom was hot and sweltering; at the far end a great fire roared beneath three or four spits which were being turned by grimy-faced lads. Kathryn and Colum took a table near the window. A sweat-soaked slattern served them pork from pigs fed on the tenderest of acorns, and slices of carp, sharp in their tangy sauce, as well as watered wine in wooden bowls. Down the middle of the tavern was a great grease-covered table where the rest of the customers, most of them pilgrims, waited for the cook to bring down the meat on the spit so they could cut off slices. Colum watched this for a while. Now and again he glanced at Kathryn, noticing how deftly and delicately she cut her meat and popped small morsels into her mouth, afterwards washing her fingers daintily in a bowl of water and dabbing them on a napkin. She would do well at court, Colum thought. Kathryn looked up.

'What are you thinking about, Irishman?'

'I am sorry I lost my temper over Brantam.' Colum sipped from his wine-bowl. 'I must remember I am not in camp.' He stared at her. 'I am inconsiderate; it must be difficult being a woman physician. I mean with people like Cotterell!'

'Such people have the difficulty. I have none at all.'

'Why did you forsake your husband's name?'

Kathryn shrugged. 'Why does everyone ask me that?' She stared down the tavern, where two cats were fighting over a rat they had caught. 'My husband's gone. I am a widow.' Kathryn sighed. 'Well, to all intents and purposes, I am.'

'Though his body has never been found?'

Kathryn looked at him and Colum knew he had touched her to the quick, for her eyes were guarded.

'Let's leave that matter, Colum,' she replied.

'The business at the Guildhall,' Colum continued, so as to hide his embarrassment. 'Do you have any suspicions?'

Kathryn leaned back against the wall. She felt hot and tired. She wanted to return to Ottemelle Lane rather than sit in this sweltering tavern, with the cloth of her gown clinging to her body.

'The murderer is an educated man,' she said, 'who knows Canterbury and has a grievance against the shrine. But what happens if we are wrong about the rest, eh,

Irishman? What if he's a physician not on Newington's list?'

'Newington is thorough.'

'Fine, fine, but what happens if it is someone who simply has access to medicines and potions?' Kathryn picked up her wine-bowl. 'It might be easier if we hired men to watch all our suspects.'

'That's impossible,' Colum said. 'We have no right to do so, and we would be levelling an accusation against them which we can't prove. As physicians they can go where they wish. As you said, even at night they have keys to the postern gates. If they are determined enough, they could give any spy the slip, so that would avail us nothing.'

Colum leaned over and squeezed her hand. 'You have already earned your fee, Mistress Swinbrooke, with this business of the poet Chaucer.'

'We shall take it further,' Kathryn returned, 'when Luberon sends the Archbishop's copy to my house. Which reminds me, Irishman, I should be grateful if you would ask them to send me a copy of the indenture and the fee the Corporation owes me.' Kathryn cleaned her fingers with the napkin. 'A poor patient not paying his fee is one thing, the Corporation of Canterbury is another! Now I must go.'

Colum insisted on paying the taverner's fee, drained the dregs from his cup and gestured at Kathryn to remain seated.

'Mistress, I have a favour to ask.'

Kathryn looked askance.

'The manor at Kingsmead . . .' Colum stammered. 'The floors are rotten, the window shutters broken and the roof has as many holes as a net. I wondered . . .'

'You wondered what?'

'I wonder if I could rent a chamber in your house? At least until the manor is fit to live in.'

Kathryn stared at him.

'I could pay good silver,' he added.

Kathryn gazed coolly at him. The Irishman looked like a boy asking a favour of his mother. If I refuse, Kathryn thought, I will give great offence, but if I accept . . . ? She thought of Thomasina, her resolute protector.

'Agreed,' she smiled.

'Thank you. I shall see Luberon and move my baggage down tonight.'

'Then, Irishman'—Kathryn rose—'I bid you adieu.'

Thomasina, huffing and puffing, two bundles of long, yellowing rushes under her arm, walked up Ridinggate towards Ottemelle Lane. Rawnose the pedlar was standing at the corner.

'You have heard the news, Mistress?'

Thomasina looked at the poor beggar's face. He was a veritable nuisance, but his injuries were so terrible, every time she looked at him she felt a surge of compassion.

'No, Rawnose,' she said wearily, 'I have not heard the news.' She bought a tawdry trinket from the tray slung round his neck.

'Well, well,' Rawnose gabbled. 'They have hunted the Lancastrians down, their last general, Falconberg, has had his head cut off and stuck on a pole over London Bridge. They say Faunte is hiding in the woods outside Canterbury, and someone else has been poisoned, a merchant. Widow Gumple wants to be the leader of the next parish council.' On and on he rambled till Thomasina, her arms growing tired with the heavy rushes, just left him talking and walked farther down the street. She saw a man bending over a pewterer's stall and recognised the fat buttocks of the pompous Goldere. Thomasina smiled, moved the rushes further along her arm and hurried past, making sure the sharp edges of her bundles clipped the well-dressed hose. Goldere sprang up.

'Ooh! Ooh!' he cried.

Thomasina stopped. 'I am so sorry,' she said breathlessly. 'I'm in such a hurry!' And grinning from ear to ear, she walked back to the Swinbrooke house.

Agnes let her in. After Thomasina had told her what gossip she thought Agnes should know, they cleared the old rushes from the kitchen, swept the floor and laid down new ones, sprinkling them with mint and thyme. Thomasina anxiously wondered where Kathryn was. She didn't trust the Irishman and she was frightened that her mistress might become caught up in the toils of the men of power. She only lent half an ear to Agnes's chatter until the young girl suddenly went quiet, letting the broom slip out of her hand.

'Oh, I am sorry! I am sorry!' Agnes exclaimed. 'I forgot; a letter arrived for Mistress Kathryn!'

She hurried out to Kathryn's small chancery office and came back with a piece of parchment, dirty and soiled but sealed with a blob of wax. Thomasina wiped her hands on the front of her gown and fairly snatched it from the girl.

'I'll take care of that!' she snapped and bustled out of the kitchen up the stairs to her own chamber. She locked the door firmly behind her and sat down on the quilted cover of the large four-poster bed, a gift from her father on her first wedding morn.

'The sights you have seen!' Thomasina murmured.

She laughed and cried a little, wiping the tears from her eyes. She always did that whenever she sat on the bed and recalled the past. Then she examined the piece of parchment. Something was wrong with her mistress, and these mysterious letters always seemed to make matters worse. Thomasina fingered the red wax. Something was amiss. Something to do with that terrible bastard of a husband, Alexander Wyville. Thomasina had been so glad when he had left a day earlier than he'd planned. She brooded over what had happened. She had taken Kathryn to physician Swinbrooke's kinsman Joscelyn to stay the night. When they returned Kathryn's father simply announced Alexander had gone: he had packed his belongings, cleared the money from his chest, taken the sword, buckler and spear he had bought and gone to join Faunte's levies massing in the fields near St Dunstan's Church outside Westcliff. Kathryn had never been the same since, whilst her father had begun to sink deeper into a pit of depression.

Thomasina pursed her lips, breathed deeply through her nose, then broke open the seal and undid the letter. She had glimpsed the scrawled handwriting on a previous note, now she flinched at the malice in the message: 'Where is your husband? Where is Alexander Wyville? Murder is a crime and murderers hang!'

Thomasina studied the crudely drawn gibbet and the long-haired woman hanging from it, followed by the words penned beneath: 'But silence is golden and the gold can be left, three pieces, on Goodman Theodore's grave in the corner of Saint Mildred's Churchyard. Today between the fourth and fifth hour.'

Thomasina screwed the letter up into a ball and hurried down to the kitchen. She looked at the hour-candle. The flame had already eaten away the fourth ring. Thomasina threw the malicious note into the fire and watched it turn to ash.

'Agnes!' she shouted. 'Agnes, come here!'

The young girl hurried up, her thin face tense with the excitement she now felt in the house: Mistress Kathryn going here and there; lecherous Irishmen being invited to supper; mysterious notes; and now Thomasina red-faced and agitated. The maid grabbed Agnes by the shoulder.

'Listen, girl, you like sugared comfits?'

Agnes nodded.

'And you'd like a bowl of them?'

Again Agnes nodded.

Thomasina pointed dramatically at the buttery. 'They are in there, all for you, on one condition. You are not to tell Mistress Swinbrooke about that note! Do you understand?'

Agnes crossed her heart and swore to die if she broke her promise. Thomasina squeezed her shoulder once more and bustled out of the door, whilst Agnes sped like an arrow to the buttery and the reward for her silence. Thomasina hurried down Ottemelle Lane, knocking aside Mollyns the miller, who tried to stop her. Goldere got another shove, whilst poor Rawnose didn't even have time to open his mouth as Thomasina swept into Hethenman Lane down past the hospital. Above her rose the iron-bound gates, the crenellated turrets and lofty towers of Canterbury Castle, and to its left the tall, elegant spire of St Mildred's Church where it stood on a small hill above the river Stour.

Although Ottemelle Lane was on the border of the parish of St Margaret's, Kathryn's family had always worshipped at St Mildred's. Old Father Matthews was parish priest, a holy man who had officiated at the last of Thomasina's marriages; now he had grown too weak to withstand the mighty Widow Gumple who, with her accomplices, intended to make the church her own preserve. Thomasina just hoped she was in time. Whoever was sending Mistress Kathryn those notes would wander into the graveyard, and Thomasina intended to be there. She walked through the lych-gate into what the people called God's Acre. She crossed herself and said the Requiem for her own parents, brothers and sisters, not to mention two of her husbands and four of her still-born babies, who were all buried there. Thomasina's usually stout cheery face drained of colour. She looked over to the greystone wall of the church, counting the windows along the northern transept. When she got to number six she looked down and, though the grass was overgrown, she glimpsed the small weather-stained stone crosses.

'Oh, my little ones,' she whispered.

She stared round. She must not think of them, otherwise she would cry and crumble, and she had to be strong. She peered between the stout yew-trees, their branches bending to meet the overgrown grass and gorse.

'If the bastard comes,' Thomasina muttered, 'I'll catch him!'

She strained her ears, but all she heard was the chirping of the birds and the buzzing song of the grasshoppers. Beautiful butterflies hovered above the wild-flowers, and once again she thought of the souls of her little babies. Did the butterflies represent them? She drew in her breath and followed the beaten track through the cemetery into the far corner where Goodman Theodore's tomb, a large weather-beaten marble affair, lay cracking under the hot sun. The tomb was well-known in the parish as a trysting place for young lovers. 'So many memories,' Thomasina said to herself. An eternity ago she had met Father Cuthbert here, when he was a novice, not yet fully consecrated to the Church. They had stood over there near the old yew-tree, young and innocent under a hunter's moon, whilst the stars had winked like jewels against a dark velvet sky.

Thomasina wiped her eyes and moved across to the yew-tree. Its trunk had been split by a tongue of lightning many storms ago. She concealed herself carefully behind it and watched the path to Goodman Theodore's tomb. Thomasina must have stood for a good half-hour, torn between a desire to catch the man blackmailing her mistress and the torment of remembering the bitter-sweet dreams this place provoked in her soul. Birds swooped and sang above the tombs. A battered tom-cat slipped through the grass hunting for voles and shrews. A young couple came in and lay down on the hot grass, twisting and turning in their passionate embraces. When Thomasina coughed, they rose and scuttled off as fast as rabbits, but no one else came.

At last Thomasina heard the side door of the church open and Widow Gumple came out. She looked so ridiculous in a yellow gown and a high-horned head-dress that Thomasina had to stifle her giggles. Widow Gumple's fat, vinegarish face glowered around the cemetery, almost as if she suspected someone was lurking there, then she went back into the church, slamming the door behind her. Thomasina sighed. The blackmailer hadn't come, so she wearily made her way home.

In the yard of the Fastolf Inn just outside Westgate, Thopas, the assassin, sat on a bench warming himself in the late-afternoon sun and watched the stream of pilgrims arrive. He pulled the cowl closer over his head as he hungrily surveyed this new batch of possible victims, feeling a surge of power, like wine, in his veins. He was lord of life and death. He would carry out judgement against Becket's shrine and the city for the death of his mother. He leaned back, cradling the leather blackjack of ale in his hand, eyes half-closed as he listened to the clatter of hooves, the trundle of carts on the cobbles, the shouts of ostlers and the cries of customers seeking attention. He sniffed the warm air, the pungent smell of horse manure mixed with the more savoury smells from the large cone-shaped kitchen which served the hostelry. A lame beggar hopped like a frog towards the door of the inn. A nun, fashionable in her pink lace-edged wimple, lifted her skirts and thick white petticoats, her little nose wrinkling at the smells. She talked in a nasal French accent to the sister trotting beside her. Thopas studied the woman, arrogant, well-dressed, courtly and refined. There was very little there of the law of Christ or the vow of poverty. A possible victim? Thopas wondered. Then he heard a loud braying voice.

'Make way! Make way for John atte-Southgate, Lord High Summoner in the Archdeacon's court of the Bishop of London!'

Thopas moved on the bench and studied the summoner carefully. A true bastard of Satan, he thought, with his scrawny black hair, pot-belly, jutting unshaven jaw, high rubicund cheeks and the darting eyes of an angry sow. Thopas looked at the fellow's well-heeled Spanish-leather riding-boots, the costly belt round his beer-belly, his long cloak trimmed with squirrel fur and the ponderous saddle-bags full of writs and summonses. A human kite, Thopas thought: a church lackey who went round digging out people's sins before summoning them into the Archdeacon's court: the man who didn't pay his tithes, the parish priest who had a lady friend, the curate absent from his living. Men like Southgate were paid by the Church for serving writs but they accepted bribes from those who could afford to buy them off.

Thopas's quarry, John atte-Southgate, threw the reins of his horse at an ostler and, with his saddle-bags flung over his arm, strode into the Fastolf Inn, a man fully aware of his power. He saw the elegant nun shy away and the hedge-priest from Somerset scuttle into the taproom's darkness like a frightened mouse. Southgate smiled. It had been a good year and he was right to give thanks to the shrine and, who knew, amongst the many pilgrims he might find business. Perhaps a cleric who had brought a lady friend? Or that nun; should she have left her convent? Southgate grinned evilly and he bellowed for wine, the best in the house, totally unaware of the demand made for his soul.

Kathryn arrived back at Ottemelle Lane to find Thomasina poring over the household accounts. Her maid looked rather pink-faced and refused to meet Kathryn's eyes and Kathryn wondered if she was still sulking over Colum. Agnes brought a stoup of watered ale and slices of white bread laid out on a trencher. Kathryn sat at the top of the table nibbling the bread whilst Thomasina, still studying the accounts, mumbled and muttered to herself.

'What's the matter, Thomasina?'

The maid looked up, her brown-berry eyes bright with excitement.

'Nothing, nothing.'

'Thomasina, I know you too well!'

Thomasina put down the quill and glared at Agnes, who was peeping round the corner of the kitchen.

'Nothing's wrong,' she said flatly. 'In fact, we are showing a slight profit. Even more so when Lord Luberon sends us a copy of the indenture and the first payment of your fee. And yes, I, too, have known you years, Mistress, even before your mother died,' she added, trying to divert the conversation.

'What was she like, Thomasina?'

The maid sighed. Kathryn always asked this question and Thomasina always gave her the same reply.

'You were a babe, my sweet, but you would have loved her. She was very like you, tall and elegant. Her hair was black as night and her eyes were soft and kind. No man loved a woman as passionately as your father did your mother, he never married again. Never!'

Thomasina stared down at the table and Kathryn wondered for the umpteenth time if Thomasina, this woman of prodigious appetites and deep passion, had been in love with her father.

'Do you like him?' Thomasina asked abruptly.

'Oh, the Irishman?' Kathryn asked.

Thomasina looked up quickly. Kathryn shrugged and pushed the trencher away.

'He's a strange one.'

'No,' Thomasina added, quietly enjoying the trap she had set. 'I meant Chaddedon!'

Kathryn remembered the dark sardonic face of the doctor, blushed and got to her feet.

'I have news for you, Thomasina. The Irishman is going to stay here.'

And ignoring her maid's shrill imprecations, Kathryn fled for safety into her writing-office.

Outside in the kitchen Thomasina, now joined by Agnes, loudly bemoaned the dangers of having an Irish cut-throat sleeping in the house. Kathryn laughed softly at the thrill of excitement in Thomasina's voice. She thought of Chaddedon but shook her head. She had other business to deal with. She looked where her father had kept his books and took down Gaddesden's *Rosa Anglica.* Buckler's wife would be returning soon and Kathryn wanted to know what the authority said about pregnancy, so she would be well prepared. She sat scanning the yellowing pages until she heard a knock on the door and Thomasina's voice welcoming the visitor into the house. The woman edged her way into the kitchen, as if she was reluctant to be there. She was dressed as she had been earlier in the day, though Kathryn noticed she had drawn the veil more closely over her face. Kathryn sat the woman down and studied her, then stretched forward and carefully lifted the veil to reveal an angry bruise just under the woman's right eye.

'You did not have that this morning.'

Mathilda Buckler looked away.

'I slipped and fell,' she stuttered.

'No, you didn't,' Kathryn replied. 'Your husband struck you.' She looked up at Thomasina, who was standing behind Mathilda. 'A piece of raw meat, Thomasina, crushed and dried.'

Thomasina hurried into the buttery and brought the meat back, a piece of steak cut off from a leg of venison, which had been hung to cure there.

'Hold it against your eye,' Kathryn ordered. 'God knows why, but it will lessen the bruise. When you return home, wash it frequently in warm water mixed with rose-petals and a juice distilled from witch hazel. I will give you a small phial of it. Whatever you do, especially after applying the meat, keep the bruise clean. Do you understand?'

The woman nodded.

'Your husband struck you, didn't he?'

Again the woman nodded.

'I feel ridiculous,' Mathilda said. 'This piece of meat.'

'You'd look even worse with that bruise showing. Hold it there for a while. Now, why did your husband strike you?'

'He says I am barren.'

'And are you?'

'I don't know!' Mathilda cried. 'I have been his wife for a year, and Mistress, I have tried so hard!'

'Do you have sisters?'

'Yes, four.'

'Are they married and do they have children?'

'Yes, yes, they do, but my husband scorns me, and his kinsfolk look down on me.' Mathilda took the meat away from her eye. 'Mistress, what can I do? I am a good wife and in the bedchamber I try hard to please my husband.'

'Does he love you?'

Mathilda looked away. 'He wants an heir.'

'And is your husband potent?'

Now Mathilda blushed. 'It's not his fault,' she whispered. 'He drinks too much and sometimes the . . .'

'The coitus,' Kathryn continued. 'The union is not complete?'

Kathryn stared at the girl and tried to hide her pity. Such cases were common. A drunken husband, suffering from what her father had always called the "miller's droop," impotent himself but beating his wife like a thug. She knew no medical examination could tell for sure but noted the generous, swelling breasts of the girl, her slim waist and broad hips.

'You will have many children,' Kathryn told her.

'Mistress, is there some potion I can take? Or give my . . .' her voice faltered.

'Give your husband?' Kathryn added. 'Lady Mathilda, I beg you, steer clear of such philtres. They can do more harm than good. Many a woman has stood trial for her life for wrongfully poisoning her husband.'

Mathilda stared at her. 'Is there nothing?'

Kathryn touched the woman's cheek gently with her finger. 'I am a physician, Lady Mathilda, not a liar. It is your husband who should change, be less quick to fill his cup, be more patient when he's drunk.' Kathryn looked despairingly over at Thomasina, who just shrugged. 'Come back,' Kathryn urged. 'Come back in a few days. Let me think.'

Thomasina went and fetched the phial of witch hazel. Kathryn refused any payment and watched the woman leave. She waited till the door closed behind her.

'What can I do?' she pleaded with Thomasina. 'It's a man's world, and poor Mathilda is going to learn that.'

'Isn't there anything?' Thomasina enquired.

'Such as what?' Kathryn snapped. 'Speak to Sir John Buckler, who will beat his wife even more? God damn him!'

Kathryn went back to her writing-office, where she sat glaring at the wall. She was still in a temper when Colum arrived, cheery-faced, a saddle-bag slung across each shoulder, another linked over his arm. He walked into the kitchen, his face slightly flushed, and Kathryn wondered if he had been drinking. He threw his saddle-bags down on the table, blew a kiss at Thomasina and Agnes, then undid one of the pouches.

'I bring prizes, Mistress Swinbrooke.' He handed over a small scroll serrated at the edges. 'Your indenture.' Then he gave her a small fat purse. 'And your first fee. You shall also have this, on loan from the Archbishop. You must take great care of it, I have stood security for you.' He drew out a thick calfskin-covered tome from the saddle-bag and presented it to her.

Kathryn undid the metal clasp. She looked at the title page, engraved in gilt by some long-dead clerk. *The Works of Sir Geoffrey Chaucer.* Kathryn smoothed the page with her fingers.

'I shall take good care of it. Thomasina, some wine for our visitor!'

The maid, casting black looks and talking under her breath, hurried out and returned just as quickly, as if she couldn't bear to leave the Irishman alone with her mistress. She thrust the cup at Colum so hard, the wine splashed onto his hand. The Irishman just smiled his thanks.

Kathryn went to her writing-chamber where she locked the book, indenture and purse in the great iron-barred chest, then returned to the kitchen.

'Do you bring any further news, Master Murtagh?'

She noticed the fresh glow in his face and how his eyes sparkled.

'No, but Holbech's proving to be a good taskmaster. Wood and stone have been ordered and work should soon begin at Kingsmead.'

'Have your retinue moved in there?'

'Oh, no, not yet, they are still camped with the rest down near the river Stour.' Colum was swaying slightly.

'In which case,' Kathryn snapped, 'you can tell Holbech to drink less, and the same applies to you, Master Irishman!'

Kathryn took the cup from Murtagh's unresisting hands. 'You are under my roof now and you have drunk enough wine! Some water?'

The Irishman just pulled a face, secretly pleased by Kathryn's care and fussing over him. He gratefully accepted the tankard of fresh rain-water Agnes brought for him, winked at the wide-eyed girl and sent her scuttling back to the buttery.

'One further piece of news, Mistress Kathryn,' he said. 'You, I and the fair Thomasina have been invited to sup tonight with our collegium of doctors near Queningate. Cotterell has also been invited, and Newington, being Darryl's father-in-law, will also be there.' Colum's eyes narrowed. 'They say they will answer any of our questions regarding these murders, though I think the invitation was issued by Chaddedon. He appears to be sweet on you,' Colum added mischievously.

'That's my business!' Kathryn said, trying to hide her embarrassment. 'What time are we to be there?'

'About nine.'

'Then, Irishman, I suggest you shave, wash and make yourself at home in your new quarters!'

Kathryn went to poke furiously at the embers of the fire whilst Thomasina, nose in the air, led a grinning Irishman off to his chamber.

Chapter 8

For a while Kathryn busied herself in the kitchen. She, Agnes and Thomasina went out to look at the herb gardens to ensure that the nasturtium was growing properly.

'It keeps the soil rich and free of weeds,' Kathryn explained.

She followed the path round, checking the coriander, mint, thyme, parsley, the deadly foxglove and the even more dangerous poisonous nightshade. She then returned to answer a stream of knocks on the door from patients seeking her attention. Clara, the daughter of Beton the brewer, asked for some cherry wine for her father's gout. Clement the cobbler needed a herbal poultice for a slit in his wrist. Paulina the poulterer, whom Thomasina privately thought supplemented her income with visits from young men, had to be taken to Kathryn's private chamber as she required a herbal poultice for what she called "a scratching in a most delicate part." Finally Rawnose arrived with Tim the tinker, who had been stung by a bee and the swelling had become red and sore. Kathryn gently treated him with juice of plantain whilst listening to the self-proclaimed herald of Ottemelle Lane deliver his fresh list of news.

'Oh, yes,' Rawnose said. 'The Guild of Palmers are allowing their members to go to night-watches for the dead of their Guild, provided they abstain from raising apparitions or from indecent games. Petronella of Maidstone has been convicted of mixing powders with spiders and black worms and a herb called Mil . . .'

'Milfoil?' Kathryn queried gently.

'That's it, Mistress. She used her mixture to summon up demons with the faces of women and the horns of a goat.'

On and on Rawnose chattered, whilst Kathryn wondered about the invitation to supper, a further meeting with Chaddedon, as well as what she should wear for the occasion. Thomasina clattered round the kitchen like a knight in mailed armour, filling pots with water and sending Agnes hither and thither with night-jars, blankets and bolsters for what Thomasina loudly called "that grinning Irishman."

At last Rawnose and his now more placid comrade left. Kathryn washed her hands. She would have liked to have gone to her own writing-office to look at Chaucer's book but the flame of the hour-candle was spluttering away the rings, so she helped Thomasina take pots of boiling water upstairs to the large steel-bound tub covered by a woollen cloth which stood in the corner of Kathryn's bedchamber. She and Thomasina filled the tub, adding rose-petals and lavender. Kathryn quickly stripped and washed herself, rubbing her body with Castilian soap and a hard-edged sponge her father had bought in London. She quickly dressed, choosing a satin gown of dark blue embroidered at the cuffs and around the high neck with gold satin, and went down to the kitchen. Thomasina always insisted on doing her hair, a ritual which had taken place before the fire ever since Kathryn had been a little girl. Thomasina shooed Agnes out, sending her on some errand, and brought out the silver-backed brush and comb. Thomasina undid the tresses of her mistress's hair, letting it fall like a shimmering mass of black silk down her back.

She noticed the strands of silver at the temple and tut-tutted softly to herself. She began to comb carefully, her ears straining to make sure Agnes had gone, for Thomasina had decided to seize the opportunity and confront Kathryn with what she had learnt. Kathryn half-turned and smiled.

'Come on, Thomasina. Say what you have to!'

Thomasina quickly blurted out how she had found the letter, read its filthy contents and tossed it into the fire. She then described her fruitless journey to St Mildred's graveyard.

'I did wrong, Mistress,' she concluded flatly, though her brushing of Kathryn's hair was as vigorous as ever. 'But I have known you since you were a tiny girl. So tell me, what did happen the night Alexander left?'

Kathryn just stared into the flames, soothed by Thomasina's care and the movement of the brush on her hair. She felt lulled, yet at the same time more alive than she had for years. She had been living a lie, and the presence of the Irishman, the business of the assassin, the feeling of being involved, the admiration of Chaddedon—these had pushed her out of her trance back into reality. She moved her hand, grasped Thomasina's and squeezed it gently.

'You did no wrong, Thomasina, so I'll tell you. Alexander Wyville was a young man of good looks and good family. He was the only child, and his mother, who died a year before our marriage, left him her sole heir.' She smiled over her shoulder. 'For God's sake, Thomasina, you know as much about him as I do. He was an apothecary who courted me, and my father blessed the union. Do you remember the nights we used to spend in this kitchen? Drawing up plans for opening a shop and importing herbs and spices?'

Thomasina nodded. Now was the time to keep silent, though, from the beginning, she'd had her doubts. Nothing much, just rumours of how Alexander visited the tavern opposite St Mildred's more than he did the church.

Kathryn shrugged. 'The rest you know. I married Alexander. I wanted to love him, bear his children, but he was two men. The ambitious apothecary and the drunken wife-beater.' She caught and held Thomasina's fingers resting on her shoulder. 'I knew you knew, my father knew, but we all pretended different. How could such a young man have so much hate in him? He envied my father. Then the war broke out again, and Alexander saw it as a chance to win royal favour as an apothecary, a soldier in the King's wars. He announced his intentions to join Faunte's forces outside Westgate. My father agreed. I just wanted him to go; but one afternoon, Father came to see me, white-faced, tears brimming in eyes now as hard as glass. He said he wanted Alexander dead.' Kathryn bit her lip. 'I asked why, but he muttered something about Alexander being a faithless wastrel as well as a bully.' Kathryn shrugged. 'I was too tired, too dazed to reflect on what he said. Father then insisted that you and I spend the night with his kinsman Joscelyn. Do you remember?'

She turned and looked sharply at Thomasina, who nodded.

'When we came back, my father was very quiet. He looked white-faced and dishevelled and announced Alexander had left the previous evening.' Kathryn let go of Thomasina's fingers. 'I didn't really care. Then Father became ill. On the morning he died, he asked to see me alone.'

Thomasina kept quiet; she remembered leaving physician Swinbrooke and hurrying along to Kathryn's chamber to tell her the death rattle had begun in her father's throat and that he wanted to see her alone.

'Well . . .' Kathryn rose and, lifting the hem of her gown, walked towards the door leading into the garden. 'My father confessed how he had killed Alexander!'

'Your father murdered Alexander?'

Kathryn spun round, her face drawn, her eyes dark

pools of hurt. 'Yes, murdered. He said, before God, Alexander had deserved it, and how he had confessed the same to Father Cuthbert.'

Thomasina sat down, clutching her stomach as the fear sent her heart hammering.

'For God's sake, Mistress,' she breathed, 'but where is the corpse? And those messages? They are true?'

'Aye, according to my father. You see, during the evening we were absent, Alexander had been sitting in the garden bower near the wicket gate. Father took him a cup of claret in a deep-bowled hanaper, which contained a strong infusion of valerian. The drugged wine would have sent Alexander into a sleep from which he would never awake. Father left Alexander to his sottishness and went out of the house, walking the streets until it was over. However, when he came back'—Kathryn rubbed her sweat-soaked palms together—'he found the cup lying on the grass but Alexander had gone. Now Alexander used to go to a favourite spot behind Saint Mildred's Church, beneath some willow trees overlooking the Stour River. He would always go there to sober up after he had been in his cups.'

Thomasina just nodded.

'So that evening, just before sunset, my father went there as well, but it was too late. Alexander had either slipped or fallen into the river, leaving only his cloak on the river bank.' Kathryn blinked away the tears. 'And that was all.'

Thomasina drew in her breath, breathed deeply and stared down at a stain on the front of her dress. Her mistress's story made sense. Kathryn's father had loved his daughter passionately, and though he said little to Thomasina, the maid had known how he had come to hate Alexander's cruelty and drunken ways. The feckless young man was forever going to his favourite place along the river. Indeed, Thomasina had even suspected Alexander used to meet someone there, and apparently, so had physician Swinbrooke.

'So Alexander has disappeared, yet someone must know the secret. But who, why and how?'

They both jumped as the kitchen door opened and Colum, dressed in a tawny jerkin, a brilliant white open-necked shirt and green velvet hose, walked slowly into the kitchen. He closed the door quietly behind him and threw his cherry-brown cloak over a stool. Despite her surprise, Kathryn noticed how he had taken great care over his appearance: his face was shaved and he had made some attempt to impose order on his unruly black hair. Thomasina rose like a spitting cat.

'Never trust an Irishman!' she hissed. 'Bum-boys, the lot of them!'

Colum stared at her, shook his head and bowed courteously at Kathryn.

'Mistress Swinbrooke, I apologise.' He lifted one of his soft leather boots. 'They are soft-soled and, since a lad, I tread as quietly as a ghost.' Colum drew closer, raised Kathryn's ice-cold hand and brushed it gently with his lips. 'Before God, Mistress, I did not mean to eavesdrop, but the door was off its latch.' He let her hand go and stood back to address both women. 'Yet what does it matter? So a bastard got his just deserts and now someone blackmails you.' He shrugged. 'I guessed as much. We all have secrets.' He looked hard at Thomasina. 'As I said before, what affects your mistress affects me. She is now the King's servant and, more importantly, I can help her.' He gestured with his hand and Kathryn caught the glint of the gold amulet on his wrist. 'Such a thing is not uncommon. Men disappear every day. If all the deserted wives assembled in one place, they'd form an army.' Colum looked down and sifted amongst the rushes with the toe of his boot. 'Mistress, sit down. Thomasina, fetch us some wine, heavily watered, for we have not yet eaten.'

Kathryn did so, nodding at Thomasina to obey, for the Irishman apparently bore her no malice.

Colum cleared his throat. 'Mistress, I don't think your father committed murder.'

'What?'

Colum doggedly shook his head. 'First, your husband must have survived to tell someone else. Surely, you didn't tell anyone, and apart from his confessor, your father certainly didn't.' Colum closed his eyes and remembered the soldiers' camp down near the river Stour and Holbech's list of complaints. 'Your husband's corpse, was it ever discovered?'

'Of course not. My father and I were in no position to demand an inquest!'

'But your husband's cloak was found?'

Kathryn agreed. 'I did make enquiries amongst the muster serjeants if anyone called Wyville had joined them, but they said no.'

Colum tapped the top of the table with his hand.

'Mistress, if you go farther south along the river, what do you find?'

'There are mills, dykes to create carp ponds, bridges.' Kathryn's voice trailed away and she looked up, her eyes smiling.

'Of course,' she breathed. 'Thomasina, can't you see? My father was a city physician. For months after Alexander's disappearance he made careful study of the death rolls for the body of an unnamed man being taken from the river. His search was fruitless, and though he found this strange, my father always accepted it because of his guilt.' She fingered the gold embroidery on the neck of her gown. 'Master Irishman, you must be right. The Stour is fast-flowing; one of the mills or bridges would have caught and held Alexander's corpse. But the valerian?'

Colum shrugged. 'You are the physician, Mistress. Did he drink all of it, or just some of it? Did he gulp it down and retch it up again? I tell you this, Mistress Swinbrooke:

your husband did not drown, and you may well not be a widow.'

Kathryn suddenly went cold. 'Alexander,' she breathed, 'might return!'

Kathryn stared down at the table, guilty at the lies she had been feeding herself. On the one hand, her father had confessed to murdering her husband, but to counter that Kathryn had encouraged the belief that Alexander may have met with an accident, drowned himself or just absconded, and would never come back. Whatever had happened, she had comforted herself with the thought that Alexander would not return. Kathryn had never faced the possibility that he might. She clutched Thomasina's hand.

'Alexander could still be here in Canterbury!' Kathryn laughed sharply. 'He could be the murderer!'

Her agitation grew so marked, Thomasina had to pull at her hand, even as the seed of an idea began to flower in her own mind.

'Hush, Mistress, the Irishman'—Thomasina beamed beatifically at Colum—'probably for the first time in his life, makes sense. Your father was no murderer. Wyville has probably left and gone to make his fortune, and if he returns, you can seek an annullment in the Church courts, but I don't think he will!' Her eyes pleaded with those of Kathryn. 'Can't you see, Mistress? The blackmailer knows Alexander will never return; otherwise those filthy messages would not be sent.'

Colum agreed, and despite her shock, Kathryn smiled at how these two were allying themselves in a friendship more unique than that between Pilate and Herod. Agnes's return from her errand ended the conversation. Colum went out into the garden, and Thomasina had a list of instructions for Agnes, so Kathryn sat for a while reflecting on what she had learnt. She derived some peace from facing the truth behind Alexander's disappearance and her father's murderous anger against him. And the blackmailer? Kathryn dismissed him; he would either grow tired or reveal himself for what he was, a criminal not to be feared.

At last Thomasina, chattering like a magpie, persuaded her mistress to return to her chamber, where Kathryn put on her hose and soft-leather brown boots, dabbed a little paint on her face and finished her preparations. Doors were locked, instructions issued to a sleepy-eyed Agnes, and then the three walked into Ottemelle Lane. They went up St Margaret's Street through the Mercery and into Burgate, shadowed by the soaring turrets, towers and gables of the cathedral. Canterbury was fairly deserted; only the muck-rakers, the night-watch and a half-drunken rat-catcher prowled the streets.

'A late time for supper,' Colum murmured, his arm now linked firmly through that of Thomasina's, whom he was gently teasing.

'But physicians are different,' he added wickedly, glancing sideways at Kathryn, who walked serenely beside him. 'They can sup late on the fruits of their wealth.'

Thomasina caught his mood and pointed to the soldier's gold amulet. 'At least our wealth is well-earned, Master Murtagh. Not fleeced from that of others!'

The Irishman laughed, now in good spirits, as Thomasina's wicked tongue wagged freely. They easily found the collegium, a large timbered four-storied building in Queningate Lane with a good view of both the cathedral grounds and those of St. Augustine's Abbey. It was really three buildings formed into one, with a large porticoed entrance guarded by wooden gates. Kathryn had heard of such establishments existing in London and Paris, where physicians pooled their resources and skills to amass larger profits as well as establish greater control of their trade. Canterbury, however, was populous enough, with its own burgesses, as well as the thousands of pilgrims, that Kathryn and her father never had any reason to object to such a practice. Thomasina gazed rather enviously at the mullioned windows, the freshly painted black beams and the white gleaming plaster. Colum was equally admiring.

'God be praised!' he whispered. 'Not even in all of Dublin could such a house be found. It's true what the King says: his merchants are princes and he wants to be one of them!'

Colum rapped at the small postern gate, which was quickly opened by a porter who led them into a yard brightly lit by spluttering torches of pitch and tar fixed on iron brackets in the wall. The yard was as spacious as that of some great tavern, with outhouses, stables, storerooms and a large cone-roofed kitchen which was linked to the rest of the house by a long gallery. Behind this rose a steep red brick wall, and even from where they stood, Kathryn could hear the noise of children playing and shouting.

'That's where their garden must be,' Thomasina whispered. 'A real garden, Mistress. Why should someone who lives here carry out bloody murders?'

'You should go to London,' Colum jibed. 'The palaces there are full of assassins.'

Any further banter was abruptly curtailed by the appearance of Chaddedon and Darryl. Both men were carefully dressed in high-collared white shirts tied at the neck by a small gold chain and sleeveless gowns padded and quilted and trimmed with costly lamb's-wool against the cool night air. Darryl was formal, and his greeting muted, but Chaddedon's pleasure at seeing Kathryn was more than apparent. He kissed Thomasina warmly on the cheeks, clasped Colum's rather reluctant hand and kissed Kathryn gallantly on the fingertips. Kathryn blushed. Chaddedon's eyes were full of gentle mockery, as if he relished such teasing. He stepped back and spread his hands wide.

'You are most welcome to our humble establishment. But come, the others wait.'

Chaddedon led them into the house and along a long wood-panelled passageway into a ground-floor solar. The room was large and spacious, with leaden-paned windows, shaped in lozenges, some of them tinted with colour. A fire burning in the large canopied fireplace and candles and torches brought the room to life, making the shadows flicker against the tapestries and cloths hanging round the walls. The wealth of the house was quietly ostentatious: woollen rugs on the floor, high-backed, quilt-seated chairs, padlocked chests and cupboards, heraldic shields above the fireplace. At the far end on a small dais stood a large oaken table prepared for supper. Silver-branched candlesticks bathed the glass goblets, dishes and decanters in pools of shimmering light. A servant took their cloaks as Kathryn stared round in delight. If only her father had lived, he too might have reaped such rewards for his labours.

'The rest are waiting,' Chaddedon announced and led them over to the group who had now risen from their chairs around the fire. Straunge seemed thin and disapproving. Newington, soberly dressed, his hair groomed, his quick eyes watching everything, smiled thinly and nodded at Kathryn. Cotterell swayed dangerously on his feet, licking thick lips and looking bleary-eyed; he was already far gone in his cups. Beside him stood his wife, flaxen-haired and petite, with a pretty but somewhat sharp face. She reminded Kathryn of a doll she had once owned. Between Matthew Darryl and Newington was Marisa, the alderman's daughter. She looked like her father, with her narrow face, thin lips and quick eyes. Both women were unwelcoming, making little attempt to put Kathryn or her companions at their ease. Chairs were brought, goblets of white wine served and desultory conversation made about the weather, the pilgrims and the news from the court in London. They wondered about the whereabouts of Faunte and other rebels and Straunge gave them a description of the new stained-glass window

King Edward had commissioned for the cathedral. At last Chaddedon got to his feet and stood with his back to the fire.

'On the third Thursday of every month,' he announced, smiling at Kathryn, 'we have a tradition here. A banquet is held, guests are invited.' He waved airily towards the garden. 'The children are at liberty to play long after dark.'

Kathryn returned his smile, but the rest just stared; they knew this evening was different from any other, and even Chaddedon's good humour could not move them. He looked directly at Colum.

'Master Murtagh, you are welcome, as companion to the fair Mistress Swinbrooke as well as for being the King's Commissioner in Canterbury.' Chaddedon coughed. 'Now, we know you have questions to ask. We, or at least I, could think of no better occasion than here at our feast, as we make our final preparations for the great mystery play at Holy Cross Church.'

He coughed again and looked quickly at Darryl, who whispered to his wife. She and Cotterell's lady rose and swiftly withdrew. Darryl followed them to the door, ushering out servants, and closed the door firmly behind them. Alderman Newington rose and stood at the corner of the hearth, one arm resting on the mantelpiece; he sipped from his wine goblet and looked at Colum.

'Master Murtagh, your questions?'

Colum did not rise but stared round the group of doctors, rich and powerful men all, who could buy him and all he possessed with a pittance of what they owned. He was conscious of Kathryn sitting beside him and of Thomasina, who had made no attempt to leave. The maid now stared, hard-faced, at the alderman whose angry looks betokened that he wished Kathryn's maid were elsewhere. Colum tapped the side of his wine goblet with his fingers.

'It's been a long day,' he began. 'And the reasons for my questions are known to you all. Murders have occurred and we think the assassin must be a physician.' He held up one hand. 'I know, I know—there could be others, but, like any judge'—he emphasized the word—'I must first consider what is probable. Master Cotterell, you were called to one of the victims?'

Cotterell just shrugged and slurped from his wine goblet. Colum breathed deeply to contain his anger.

'Apart from that,' he conceded, 'there is little connection between anyone here and the victims. So let us concentrate on one fact. Yesterday, about noon, a merchant named Spurrier was murdered in the cathedral itself. So, where were you all?' Colum eased himself in his chair. 'I could ask you this singly, but it would be best if each of you answered in the presence of others. Master Cotterell, shall we begin with you?'

The fat physician, his rubicund features glistening in the candle-light, made a rude sound with his lips.

'Sir?'

'I was making calls,' Cotterell answered.

'Where?'

Cotterell smiled nervously. 'At Saint Thomas's Hospital and a house near Saint Alphege's.'

'And you can provide proof of this?'

'Yes, I can.'

'Then who in particular?'

Now Cotterell looked at Kathryn. 'I don't have to answer in public.'

Colum rose to his feet, his hand going to the dagger on his broad leather belt.

'Oh, Sir, yes, you do.'

Cotterell's eyes pleaded with Kathryn.

'Brantam was allowed his confession,' he complained petulantly like a little boy. 'Master Brantam walks out of the room and that's the last we see of him.'

'He's right,' Kathryn intervened quietly. She glanced up at Murtagh. 'I see no point in revealing secrets. If Master Cotterell wishes to speak to me alone and he is later found to be a liar, then, perhaps, we have found our assassin.'

Cotterell snorted. 'I am no assassin!'

'Oh, for God's sake!' Darryl snapped. 'I, for one, do not wish to hear Master Cotterell's petty secrets. Let him have his way!'

Chapter 9

Kathryn could see the situation becoming acrimonious. She rose.

'Master Cotterell, if you please?'

And, without further ado, she took him down the solar, out of earshot of the rest.

Cotterell swayed dangerously in front of her, his eyes bleary, his lips thick and slobbery.

'What was Brantam up to?' he slurred.

'That, Sir, is no business of yours,' Kathryn lied and made to walk back to join the rest.

Cotterell caught her gently by the sleeve.

'Brantam's a bastard!' he hissed. 'And my wife will lie for him as well as with him!' Cotterell looked over his shoulder at the rest of the group, then back at Kathryn. 'There's a young man, Robert Chirke. He owns a tenement near Saint Alphege's church. I was visiting him.' Cotterell looked away nervously. 'I don't have to say any more,' he mumbled.

'How long were you there?'

'From noon until two, three o'clock.'

'A long time to spend with a patient,' Kathryn murmured drily.

'Make of it what you will,' Cotterell whispered. 'But I see no reason for the rest to know.'

'Nor do I,' Kathryn replied. 'But be careful, Master Cotterell; the law is hard on those men who love other men, shall we say, in the full biblical sense?'

Cotterell stared at her under heavy-lidded eyes. 'And what about wives who fornicate?' He laughed. 'A pretty couple, aren't we? An adulteress and a sodomite.' His lips parted. 'I have no time for the bloody priests and their talk of Hell after death. I am in Hell now,' Cotterell pleaded. He waved a hand drunkenly. 'But what's the sodding use?'

He turned and lumbered back to his chair. Kathryn followed. She nodded at Colum, who now turned to the rest.

'Well, Sirs?'

'I can speak for all of us.' Chaddedon got to his feet. 'Yesterday afternoon we were receiving patients, and after that we all went across to Holy Cross Church to supervise preparations for the Guild play.'

'So, you were moving in and out of the house?' Kathryn asked.

'Yes, yes,' Straunge snapped. 'There were times when we were alone. We live ordinary lives,' he continued. 'I went up to the market in Burgate to buy some cloth. Master Darryl here met an acquaintance in the Red Lion Inn, whilst Chaddedon was the first to leave for Holy Cross Church.'

'I can vouch for that,' Newington interrupted. 'I called in here that afternoon.' He smiled. 'Marisa is my only daughter and her children are now my family.' He spread his hands and grinned sheepishly at his son-in-law. 'Matthew here knows there's another reason.' Newington waved a hand airily. 'This collegium represents one of my great investments. I stood surety when this house was bought.' He coughed nervously. 'Who can blame me for coming down to check that my stock is going well?'

A murmur of laughter greeted his words and Kathryn sensed how much the alderman's generosity and support was appreciated by the rest.

'So,' Colum said harshly, 'none of you can give me a full explanation of what you were doing? It's quite possible for one of you to have donned a cloak, joined the stream of pilgrims, administered the poison and disappeared.'

'Yes,' Chaddedon replied. 'All things are possible, Master Murtagh. We have talked about this amongst ourselves. Any one of us could have slipped away and committed this terrible crime and planned another. But, for God's sake, man, I still say there are others in Canterbury who could have done the same.'

'I agree,' Newington heatedly added. 'Luberon and I have named these men, but there could be others. Although," Newington concluded hastily, catching the warning glint in Colum's eyes, 'I cannot see who it could be. I have scrutinised Luberon's list. All the rest are too old, infirm, or elsewhere.'

The alderman gently drummed his fist against the fireplace and smiled. 'At the same time,' he continued, 'we cannot blame Master Murtagh or Mistress Swinbrooke. The news of these murders is now common rumour. Already the hostelries and taverns are reporting a drop in trade, and Luberon has told me that the men elected to the King's new parliament will present a petition complaining of the terrible murders being committed in this city.'

'Have you told my colleagues,' Kathryn asked, 'what we discovered this afternoon?'

Newington shook his head. 'It was not my place, Mistress.'

'What is this?' Darryl asked. 'Have you discovered something else?'

Kathryn laced her fingers together and carefully watched the faces of the physicians.

'The murderer selects his victims by profession. In itself that was a mystery until we realised that the poet Chaucer, in his *Canterbury Tales,* lists the same professions in the prologue of his poem.'

'What nonsense is this?' Darryl asked.

'Master Darryl, I think I made myself clear. Do you know the poet Chaucer or his work?'

Darryl shook his head and looked at his father-in-law. 'No, I do not. Father, do you?'

'Only the poet's name. Nothing else.'

'Master Cotterell?' Colum asked.

The physician shuffled his feet and nodded his head. 'Yes, yes. In fact, I have a copy of the *Canterbury Tales.*'

'So do we,' Chaddedon spoke up. 'Matthew, have you forgotten?' He turned to Straunge. 'Edmund, you are my witness. Last Michaelmas we were looking at a copy in our own library.'

'Well, I haven't read it!' Darryl retorted.

Chaddedon shrugged. 'Matthew, Matthew, I am not saying you have. A question was asked and I am answering it. We have a copy in our library upstairs. Both Straunge and I have read it.'

'Is it a crime now,' Cotterell bleated, 'to have read a poet's work? The poet Chaucer is well known. Many have read it, some have not. Possession of his poetry is no proof of murder.'

Kathryn shrugged. 'I agree. I simply asked a question.'

'Do you have any more such questions?' Darryl asked.

'Yes, we do,' Colum intervened. 'But let me ask them. We have an assassin who is poisoning pilgrims visiting the shrine of the Blessed Thomas. Mistress Swinbrooke believes that the murderer has a grudge against the shrine. Possibly someone who went there for a cure and was sorely disappointed. Would this apply to any of you?'

'Oh, for God's sake!' Darryl shouted and got to his feet, staring angrily at the hour-candle. 'I am hungry. It's time we feasted and not sit here whiling away the night with stupid questions!'

'Stupid they may be,' Kathryn replied, 'but they still demand an answer.'

'Sit down, Matthew,' Newington ordered. 'I think I can answer for everyone here save Master Cotterell.' The alderman hitched his robes closer about him. 'My wife, Marisa's mother, died eight years ago. A year later, Master Straunge lost both his parents during a visitation of the sweating sickness.'

'I am no different,' Chaddedon quickly interrupted. 'My wife, sickly after the birth of our only daughter three years previously, also died; followed eight months later by my own mother.'

Kathryn closed her eyes; she felt as if she was intruding on matters which really did not concern her.

'Master Cotterell?' Colum asked quickly to break the silence.

The fat physician stared back, his eyes brimming with tears.

'When the plague came,' he answered quietly, 'the old always died; I am no different from the rest. I lost my mother and an aunt. One day they were in the market together, the next they were on their deathbeds, spitting out their life-blood.' He rose and went across to fill his wine-cup. 'I have answered enough.'

His reply was echoed by the rest. Kathryn glanced quickly at Colum, wordlessly warning him that any further questions would only alienate their hosts.

Colum rose and spread his hands. 'There, our task is done. We crave pardon for any offence caused, but none was intended. Master Darryl, you are right.' Colum sniffed the fragrant odours wafting through the hall. 'My stomach believes my throat is cut!'

They all rose to their feet, chorusing approval at his remarks, though Kathryn still felt their hostility. Darryl led them out of the hall along a passageway through a side door into a long beautiful garden, lit by torchlight and thick beeswax candles under metal caps. The light bathed a broad expanse of green lawn which ran down to raised flower- and herb-beds. The air was thick with the fragrant sweet smell of roses and other flowers. Cotterell's and Darryl's wives were sitting on a wooden bench, chatting quietly and watching three children chase one another up and down the paved paths between the flower-beds.

'Your business is finished?' Cotterell's wife asked archly.

'As well as it can be,' Newington replied.

'The servants will now lay out dinner,' Darryl announced. 'Marisa, tell one of the maids to put the children to bed.'

Kathryn, eager to get away from this rather hostile group, handed her wine-cup to Colum.

'Whose children are they?' she asked.

'The two boys are mine,' Darryl replied, 'whilst the little girl, Marie, is Chaddedon's child.'

'Let me speak to them,' Kathryn asked. 'I'll bring them in.'

She walked quickly across the lawn, gently moving her neck and shoulders to relieve the strain of the recent meeting. The children stopped playing as she approached and stood watching her. Kathryn crouched at the end of the path. The little girl with blonde curls and a pretty little face was no more than a baby. The boys, both black-haired, gazed dourly at her, clasping small wooden swords in their hands.

'You have to come in,' Kathryn said quietly.

'Who are you?' one of the boys asked.

'My name's Kathryn. Kathryn Swinbrooke.'

'Are you a physician?'

'Yes, yes, I suppose I am.' She held out her hand, and the little girl grabbed her with her fingers and smiled shyly at her. 'And you are Marie?'

The girl nodded.

'Grandfather has told us about you,' the boy continued.

'He says you are a good physician but you ask silly questions.'

Kathryn smiled. 'Perhaps I do.'

'Grandfather always talks to us,' the boy said. 'Not like the rest.' He glared at the group of adults at the far end of the garden.

'Well, you'd best come in,' Kathryn repeated.

'We haven't finished our game yet.'

'What are you playing?'

The boy tapped his chest. 'My name's Arcite, and he'—he pointed to his brother—'is Palamon, and she's the Princess Emelye.'

'Well,' Kathryn said, taking the little girl by the hand, 'tomorrow is another day and even soldiers have to sleep at night.' She pointed down the garden at Colum. 'Ask him, he's one of the King's soldiers.'

The boys ran excitedly across the lawn, as swift as greyhounds. They besieged and embarrassed Colum with a string of questions until Darryl announced that enough was enough. A maid took the children away whilst the adults went in for supper.

The meal proved to be a veritable banquet: royal venison cooked in red wine, lemon juice and black pepper; boiled chicken stuffed with grapes; a salad made of parsley, sage, spring onions, garlic and rosemary. This was followed by rastons, small loaves made out of sweetened dough enriched with eggs, and honey-date slices, spiced wine, and pears in a sweet syrup. The servitors kept filling their cups. Colum drank deeply enough, but Kathryn limited herself to one cup, and between sips kept filling the goblet with water.

Cotterell soon fell asleep. At first, the atmosphere was rather formal and tense, but the wine soon proved to be a great leveller, and Colum was besieged with questions about the recent war, the politics of the court and the personalities of the King and his brothers. The Irishman cordially responded, giving graphic accounts of the recent campaign in the West Country, the summary execution of the Lancastrian generals and the King's determination to wipe out the House of Lancaster, both root and branch. He told droll stories about a soldier's life and its sharp contrast to the silken luxuries of the court. Nevertheless, he kept a wary eye on Kathryn, and Chaddedon's frequent attempts to draw her into a private conversation. At last, realising he was monopolising the conversation, he abruptly asked if they were all Canterbury born and bred.

'I'm not,' Newington expansively declared, 'but the rest are. I was born in Canterbury but was orphaned young and sent to a kinsman in London to learn the art and skill of the cloth trade. Twenty years ago I returned with my wife and little Marisa.' He glanced down at Kathryn. 'I have made my wealth both here and in London. I will not travel again. This city is the grandest in Europe.' His words were greeted with a quiet chorus of approval. 'Which is why,' he added sourly, 'these terrible murders must be stopped.'

Chaddedon, conscious that the conversation could provoke further discord, turned to Kathryn. 'You have heard of our library?' he asked. 'Would you like to see it?'

Kathryn glimpsed the humour in his eyes.

'You should,' he continued. 'Master Straunge here and I have collected many texts which even the monks of Canterbury would envy.'

Kathryn agreed and was rather relieved when Colum, who had kept a sharp ear on the conversation, abruptly invited himself, as did Thomasina, who had sat strangely silent during the entire evening, lost in her own thoughts. When the meal was over, Chaddedon and a slightly swaying Colum left the solar together, followed by Kathryn, who plucked Thomasina's sleeve.

'You have been very quiet,' she whispered. 'Is there anything the matter? Are you all right?'

Thomasina pursed her lips. 'Yes, yes. Strange folk, aren't they, Mistress? But I have just been thinking.'

'About what?'

'Oh, this and that.'

'Come on, Thomasina.'

'Be careful!' Thomasina hissed, trying to divert the conversation. 'Chaddedon has hot eyes for you. And I think the Irishman is jealous.'

Kathryn laughed softly and linked her arm through that of Thomasina.

'Perhaps it's all for the good,' she whispered.

Thomasina glared at her, though she was pleased to see the glow in her mistress's face and the sparkle in her eyes. The maid looked grudgingly at the back of the stumbling, laughing Irishman, who was going up the wooden stairs before them. Perhaps he's not such a bastard, Thomasina thought. Maybe the Good Lord sent him to bring this change about, but I'll still watch him, as well as the likes of Chaddedon.

The library the physician led them into was both opulent and well stocked. He quickly lit a long line of wax candles in a candelabrum in the centre of a wooden table, as well as the cresset torches fixed high in the wall, well away from the shelves. The room had been carpeted, the windows glazed with coloured glass; there was an alcove seat at one end and tables ranged down along one wall, above which hung more woven cloths. One entire wall, however, was taken up with shelves containing books of various sizes, some chained to the shelf, others lying stacked on top of one another. Kathryn had never seen so many books since her father had taken her to Duke Humphrey's library at Oxford. She clapped her hands and cried out in surprise.

'Are all these yours?'

Chaddedon basked in her praise. 'Well, not really. Straunge is the collector, especially of medical texts. We have Garnerius's *Tractatus de Matricibus.*' Chaddedon took a book from the shelf. 'And this is our most precious.' He laid the heavily embossed leather book on the table.

Kathryn reverently turned over the pages of a work her father had always longed to possess, Gerard of Cremona's *Chirugia.* She had seen a copy at Oxford, and the book brought memories flooding back of her father standing beside her, pointing to the paintings depicting women physicians. Kathryn turned to one of these and stroked the carefully etched drawings.

'You have seen this before, Kathryn?'

'Yes, yes, it was my father's favourite.'

'He was a good doctor?'

'My father visited Salerno and Padua and studied the physic of the Arabs.'

'And passed this knowledge on to you?'

'Yes, my father stayed a few months in Hainault, where he saw how they educated young girls. When he and my mother moved from London to Canterbury he hired a priest as my teacher, an old man from the Poor Priests' Hospital. A former scholar at the Halls of Oxford, until he was found to be infected with Wycliffe's doctrines.' She was conscious of Colum moving down the table, jealously watching her and Chaddedon.

'You said you had a copy of Chaucer?' the Irishman bluntly intervened.

'Ah, yes.' Chaddedon brought another book to the table, very similar to the one Colum had brought to Ottemelle Lane. Colum drew closer as Kathryn turned the pages over: the text had been well-thumbed, but there was nothing to indicate that the assassin had used it as a guide to select his victims. Kathryn turned a few more pages, then closed the book with a sigh.

'Nothing,' she whispered and gazed appreciatively round the library. 'I would love to come here,' she murmured. 'Perhaps when all this is over?'

'Mistress Swinbrooke, it would be an honour.' Chaddedon began to extinguish some of the candles. 'Finally,' he offered, 'may I show you where we keep our potions?'

He led them down the stairs, past the solar where the others sat chatting quietly amongst themselves, to a large room at the back of the house. Taking a key from his belt, Chaddedon unlocked the door, struck a tinder and carefully lit the oil-lamps. The room was a perfect square, the four walls covered in shelves, and along these were stacked pots and bowls, each with a parchment tag tied round its neck.

'Who goes to the library?' Colum abruptly asked before the physician could begin a conversation with Kathryn.

Chaddedon shrugged and looked narrow-eyed at the Irishman, as if he resented his presence. 'For God's sake, man, we all do!'

'And to this room?'

'Each of the physicians has a key, and there is a further key on the master ring of the house.' Chaddedon went along the shelves, tapping the bowls and jars as if they were old friends. 'We have ginger, ground elder, owl-hoof, hawthorn, hemlock, henbane, belladonna, valerian, foxglove. Enough poisons to kill the entire city.'

'Have you noticed anything untoward?' Kathryn asked, pointing to the table with its mixing bowls, scales, rods and jars.

'What do you mean?'

'Have you noticed any of the potions missing or interfered with?'

'No, nothing remarkable.'

'I did.'

Straunge appeared in the doorway. His gaunt face looked even more sallow in the flickering lamp-light.

'About a week ago,' he said, walking into the room, 'I came in here and found some white powder lying on the floor. Naturally, I was wearing gloves.' He smiled at Kathryn. 'I have a profound respect for some of these powders and believe they should never touch the skin. Anyway,' he continued hurriedly, 'I picked the powder up but it was nothing more than flour, white flour; yet that's not kept here.'

'This is the first I have heard of it,' Chaddedon said.

Straunge raised his eyebrows. 'At the time I thought it was of little consequence, but now that we are in suspicion of these deaths, I consider anything out of place.'

Kathryn gazed round the shelves. She couldn't make sense of Straunge's comment and, as in the library, she was caught between envy and admiration at what these physicians possessed.

'Where did you buy these?' she asked.

'Some we collect,' Chaddedon answered. 'Others we buy from the spice merchants in London or from our own Guild in Canterbury. Why do you ask?'

'My herbarium is a shop, nothing much, a small room at the front of my house in Ottemelle Lane. I have always dreamt of owning such stock.'

'You will need permission from the Guild.'

Kathryn winked mischievously. 'As my father said, in life all things are possible.'

They left the herbarium and joined the others in the solar. More wine was served, but Kathryn, now concerned at the sleepy look in Colum's eyes and Thomasina's restlessness, announced they really should take their leave. The ladies were cool in their farewells, making it very clear they would not object if they never saw Kathryn again. Darryl tried, without success, to rouse Cotterell, so only Chaddedon and Newington saw them to the door, the pressure of the physician's fingers on Kathryn's hand secretly conveying how much he had enjoyed the evening.

They walked back down Queningate Lane, Thomasina linking her arm through Kathryn's, whilst Colum, humming some song under his breath, walked in front, now and again dancing the odd jig, still very much under the influence of the deep bowls of claret he had drunk. Two members of the night-watch came by and told him to be quiet. Colum just laughed at them and continued past St Paul's Church, following the line of the old city wall through a broken archway and into St Margaret's Street. They passed the occasional beggar, whining for alms; a doxy in a doorway with her customer; and the crazed rat-catcher who grotesquely patrolled the streets, a long pole slung over his shoulder from which hung a freshly slaughtered line of rats and mice. Somewhere a dog howled at the full moon whilst cats fought over stinking mounds of refuse.

Kathryn was lost in her own thoughts, trying to ignore Colum's rather noisy ditty about the ladies of Dublin. They were just past the Crown Tavern, boarded and shuttered for the night, when three footpads sprang from an alley-way. They allowed Colum to pass, seeing the women as easy prey. They grabbed Kathryn by the sleeve of her dress whilst another tried to pinion Thomasina's arms behind her back. The maid lashed out with all the venom of an angry mare, giving one of the footpads a nasty crack on the shin. Kathryn struggled with her own assailant, clawing at the leather hood over his face, frightened by the glittering eyes and sour stench of the man's breath. Suddenly the man was pulled away. Kathryn was not certain of what happened, but Colum dragged the man towards him, pushing his stomach straight onto his long stabbing knife. Then the Irishman stood back, leaving the footpad to writhe and scream on the ground as his two companions gingerly edged towards him. In the light of a lantern-horn fixed on the tavern-door posts, Kathryn saw Colum was armed with a long dagger and a short dirk he had brought out from the top of his boot. The footpads, armed with pikes and sharp short stabbing knives, must have thought he was easy prey carrying no sword, and much the worse for drink. As they went forward, Colum retreated. One of the footpads rushed forward, his small pike aimed at the Irishman's crotch, the dagger sweeping towards Colum's face. Colum just ducked, knocked the pike aside, then lashed out with his dagger, causing the blood to spout from the man's neck. The other assailant had had enough; he dropped his weapons and fled back up the alley-way.

Kathryn stood staring at the fallen footpads. The one with the neck wound was already dead, but the other was clawing the ground, holding his stomach where the blood was now pumping out into a pool on either side of him.

'Shouldn't we . . . ?' Kathryn asked.

'Of course,' Colum replied. He knelt beside the fallen man, and before Kathryn could object, sliced the fellow's throat from ear to ear.

Kathryn was used to blood and the effects of violence, but Murtagh's cool detachment twisted her stomach and made her legs tremble. She clutched a still wide-eyed, panting Thomasina and, deaf to the cries of the Irishman, the two women hurried on ahead. When they reached the house, Kathryn clawed feverishly at the small bunch of keys which hung from a piece of silken cord tied round her waist, opened the door and went in. She sat Thomasina down, rekindled the fire and, going to the buttery, poured three large goblets of wine. When she heard Colum come into the kitchen, Kathryn went out, pushed a cup at him and took the tray across to Thomasina. The maid had now regained her composure. She gulped the wine, peering over her shoulder at the Irishman, who just slouched against the table.

'What did you expect me to do?' he demanded. 'They were footpads—soldiers, by the look of them, from the camp.' He slammed the wine-cup down on the table and went over to confront Kathryn. 'Look at me, woman!' he demanded.

Kathryn stared coolly back. 'I'm looking, Irishman!'

'They were villains,' Colum persisted. 'They would have killed me, raped you, then gutted you from crotch to neck!'

'You kill so expertly.'

Colum pushed his face closer. 'Lady, they were trying to kill me. One took it in the throat, the other had a belly wound. And not even you, never mind Chaddedon and the rest, could have done a damn thing for him! He would have taken hours to die and screamed every second for a drop of water.'

'He's right,' Thomasina declared. 'They were born bastards and they died bastards! What do you think they were after, Mistress, the time of day?'

Colum smiled and patted Thomasina on the shoulder. The maid shrugged him off.

'Keep your hands to yourself, Irishman! I am no Helen of Troy, and if I was, you're no bloody Paris!'

Colum, bellowing with laughter, picked up his wine-cup and moved towards the kitchen door.

'Irishman!'

'Yes, Mistress Kathryn?'

'I am sorry. I am grateful for what you did. You were just so cold, so callous.'

Colum walked back towards her.

'I am a man of violence, Mistress. I was born fighting. I live by fighting. I did not like what I did, but it had to be done.'

'And in the alley-way outside the Chequers, when you heard that Irish voice? Why then? What is your secret, Irishman?'

Colum made a face.

'No great secret. Years ago I ran wild with a rebel band in the glens outside Dublin.' Colum snorted with laughter. 'We called ourselves the Hounds of Ulster. We were roaring boys, hot for the blood of the English. Then one day I was caught, betrayed by a traitor and sent to the gallows. The present King's father, the Duke of York, Lord Lieutenant of Ireland, had mercy on me and I was pardoned. I forgot my past. My problem is my past has not forgotten me. The Hounds of Ulster now judge me as a traitor.' He looked down at his wine-cup. 'They fixed a price on my head. A bag of gold for its taking. It's only a matter of time, Mistress, before someone tries to collect it.' He smiled. 'If they can.'

Kathryn sighed and gestured at him to sit down. 'I am sorry,' she repeated. She sipped from her wine-cup. 'Now the evening is ruined.' She glanced quickly up at Thomasina. 'I have never seen you so quiet.'

The maid nodded at the Irishman. 'When he's around I keep my hand on my purse and my lips shut.'

'But your ears open?' Colum teased. 'And what did we discover tonight?' He ticked the points off on his fingers. 'The Cotterells are a strange couple. He strikes me as a boy-lover and she's hot-eyed. Chaddedon is charming.' He winked at Thomasina. 'Straunge and Darryl are a pair of cold fish. Newington's enigmatic. We were their guests, but we did not like them. What else?'

'I think the murderer was in that house,' Kathryn replied. 'I have no proof, just suspicions. They have a copy of Chaucer's *Tales,* but it's Straunge's remark which intrigues me. Why should he find flour on the floor of the herbarium?'

'Anything else?' Colum asked.

Kathryn shook her head wearily. 'Sufficient unto the day is the evil thereof. Thomasina, Master Murtagh, I bid you good night.'

And, leaving the Irishman and her maid to their own devices, Kathryn took her goblet of wine down to her writing-office. She lit the candles, and as she closed the door, she heard Thomasina exchanging good-natured banter with Colum, then a scrape of stools as they both retired. Kathryn just sat and stared at the wall, whilst different images and memories of the evening flitting through her mind. Chaddedon's courtesy, the opulent library, the hard-eyed women, Straunge standing in the doorway making his strange pronouncement. And lastly, the footpads leaping from the darkness and Colum's cold despatch of two of them.

Kathryn sighed and pulled across the copy of Chaucer's *Canterbury Tales.* She opened the book and began to leaf through the pages. First the Prologue, with the poet's deft touches in conveying the character and calling of each of the pilgrims, then the stories themselves. Kathryn felt a little cold, so she wrapped her cloak around herself and took the book back into the kitchen, where she lighted candles and raked up the embers of the fire. She sat with the book in her lap leafing through the different tales as this merry band of pilgrims made their way to Canterbury. She grew heavy-eyed but suddenly a line from "The Knight's Tale" caught her attention: "Two young knights sprawled together . . ." She read the succeeding verses carefully, closed the book and sat back rocking it gently in her lap. Now she had the proof. She had no doubt that she had met the assassin, the slayer of pilgrims.

Chapter 10

Despite the late hour in retiring to bed, Kathryn had intended to rise early. Instead she and the rest of the household were rudely awakened by a loud banging on the door just after dawn. Protesting at the clatter, she wrapped herself up in a cloak, slipped her feet into thonged sandals and hurried down the stairs, even as Thomasina answered the front door and ushered their visitor into the house. Colum, half-dressed and equally heavy-eyed, came crashing down the stairs after her.

'What is it?' he asked.

The cowled figure in the kitchen drew back his hood.

'For God's sake, Luberon,' Colum snarled, 'what is the matter?'

Luberon handed him a piece of dirty parchment. Murtagh studied it and passed it to Kathryn.

'There's been another murder, hasn't there?'

Luberon nodded. Kathryn studied the scrawled writing.

A summoner to Canterbury his way did trot,
And now in Hell his soul will rot.

'A summoner has been killed?' Kathryn queried.

The clerk nodded. 'John atte-Southgate in the Fastolf

Inn outside Westgate.' Luberon rubbed his unshaven cheek. 'You've got to come now. Not only has a summoner been murdered, but the whore who was with him.' Luberon sank down onto a stool. 'This good summoner, like many of his ilk, enjoyed the pleasures of life. The innkeeper says a woman, cloaked and hooded, arrived at the tavern long after curfew looking for Southgate. The taverner didn't object, he guessed she was a whore, and who would dare confront a summoner?' Luberon licked his lips. 'Apparently, they had a fine old time except that the whore brought a sealed jug of wine which contained poison. They both drank and both now lie murdered.'

'Who found the bodies?'

'A chambermaid,' Luberon replied. 'On the orders of the Archbishop, I had already ordered every taverner in the city to inform me of any sudden deaths. I was rudely awakened by an ostler with the news and came immediately here.'

'You want us to go with you?'

Luberon stood up. 'Of course!' he snapped. 'I'm not here for the good of my health!'

Colum cursed and banged the top of the table. 'But I have business out at Kingsmead. The manor is deserted. I and my merry band of men need to go to outlying farms to buy oats, bran, straw and hay for the King's horses! The horses will soon be in Canterbury and it's prudent to buy such foodstuffs as soon as possible.'

'If this matter is not settled,' Luberon snarled, 'you will have more to explain to his Grace the King than the lack of bran and oats! Get dressed!'

'Go to hell!' Colum growled.

'Colum, we must go!' Kathryn intervened. 'We have no choice.'

Kathryn returned to her chamber, dressed quickly and, when Thomasina came up, gave her maid swift instructions about what to do should any patients call.

'Tend to the herb gardens,' Kathryn added. 'The sun has been hot and the plants need watering. Deal with any cuts and bruises, but as for anything more serious, just let me know on my return.' Kathryn nudged her maid gently on the arm. 'Thomasina, for God's sake, are you with me?'

The maid's cheery face broke into a smile. 'Ah, you go, Mistress, all will be well here. Agnes and I will cope. Especially'—her voice rose—'as the house will be free of foot-clopping soldiers!'

Kathryn and Colum joined Luberon downstairs. She went and took three manchet loaves from the buttery.

'We can break our fast on these,' she said, offering the small loaves. Chewing the fine bread, they left the house. Colum hurried across the street to the corner tavern, where he had stabled his horse. He was gone some time, leaving Luberon, who had unhitched his sorry-looking nag from a nearby post, to fume and mutter curses. At last Colum returned, not only leading his own horse but a gentle cob for Kathryn. He tossed the reins at her.

'It's my gift to you,' he said, smiling. 'She's quiet, pleasant and even-tempered. Just like Thomasina!' He eschewed her thanks, saying it was part-payment for her hospitality, cupped his hands and helped Kathryn to mount. Moments later they followed Luberon out of Ottemelle Lane, along Hethenman Lane, turning left into King's Bridge, past St Peter's Gate, the Friars of the Sack and down the main thoroughfare to Westgate.

As they rode, Colum told Luberon about the previous evening's supper with the physicians. The little clerk listened sourly and became so morose at having been excluded from the invitation that Colum shrugged and fell silent, leaving Luberon to his own dark thoughts.

The city was still quiet, with only a few roisterers returning home, singing and laughing, intent on evading the watch. Colum looked at them, shamefacedly remembering his own revelry, and winked apologetically at Kathryn. They passed a forger firmly padlocked in the stocks at the mouth of Black Griffin Alley and two tinkers pushing their hand carts towards the Buttermarket. A few sleepy-eyed beadles, staves in their hands, were walking towards the soaring towers and crenellated turrets of Westgate. Kathryn studied them and abruptly reined in. Luberon turned in exasperation, pulling his horse's head round.

'What is the matter, Mistress?' he said. 'There's a corpse to be viewed and a murderer to be hunted! Are you day-dreaming?'

'Oh, be still!' Colum bellowed. 'Kathryn, what is it?'

Kathryn pointed to Westgate. 'The beadles ensure the gates of the city are shut at curfew, yes?'

Luberon nodded.

'And yet the whore arrived at the Fastolf after curfew. So who let her through?'

'The city guards certainly wouldn't,' Colum replied. 'They are King's men.'

Kathryn patted her horse's neck and gently urged it forward. 'In which case,' she concluded, 'our young lady of the night must have gone through a postern gate, and the only persons who have keys to the gate are physicians.'

'Which brings us,' Luberon declared, 'back to the beginning. But who, Mistress Swinbrooke, who?'

He led them on through Westgate, where Colum stopped to make a few enquiries of the Captain of the Guard. The grizzled soldier shook his head and pointed at the iron-bound gates.

'I locked them myself last night, and no one, especially a whore, went anywhere near them.'

Colum, shaking his head, led them out under the lowering archway, along the trackway from where they could see the gaudily painted sign of the Fastolf swinging gently in the breeze. Kathryn eased the cramp in the nape of her neck. She smelt the sweet tang of summer from the green lush fields on either side and realised how rarely she had left Canterbury since her father's death.

The Fastolf Inn was eerily quiet, the great cobbled yard empty of horses, sumpter-ponies and ostlers. Only a few soldiers, their livery rather stained and ragged, slouched against the wall. They recognised Colum, who shouted friendly abuse until a dirty-faced serjeant, thin as a bean-pole, lurched unsteadily out of one of the outhouses, a wineskin in his hand.

'We've told all the buggers to stay indoors!' he slurred. He looked evilly at Luberon. 'At least until the officials are finished.'

Colum and his small party dismounted, the Irishman throwing the reins of his horse at the serjeant. 'Take care of these!'

Kathryn and Luberon followed him across the yard into the musty taproom. The landlord, his leather apron covered in greasy spots, came bobbing and curtsying, as if Colum were the King himself. Over his shoulder Kathryn glimpsed the anxious faces of the maids, scullions and pot-boys.

'Where's the corpse?' Luberon demanded, pushing his way forward.

The landlord jabbed a dirty stubby finger at the smoke-blackened ceiling. 'In the chamber at the top. Honest to God, we haven't touched anything!'

Luberon led them up the rickety stairs. He stopped on the small second landing. 'These stairs are bloody dangerous!' he bawled down at the landlord. 'Get them fixed or I'll send the ale-tasters round!' He glowered at Colum. 'Nothing is what it should be,' Luberon grumbled. 'Bloody wars and fighting have stopped good commerce.' He seized a thin-shouldered pot-boy trying to sneak downstairs. 'Show us the chamber where the corpse is!'

The boy nodded and led them on. Kathryn had to cover her nose against the dank stench of the place. The plaster on the walls was peeling, doors to chambers hung slightly askew and the cracked windows were covered in bits of parchment. They reached the top floor of the tavern, where the boy led them down a small corridor and pointed grimly at a door. Luberon pushed it open and went in. The chamber was nothing but a lime-washed box. The walls were covered with dark stains. The rushes on the floor were dry and hard, as if they had not been changed for years, and Kathryn grimaced at the dog turds nestling there. The bed was a massive, derelict four-poster, curtained off by ragged draperies. Luberon pulled these aside and Kathryn flinched at the sight of the two corpses which lay there. On one side of the bed the summoner was naked as the day he was born, the fat flesh on his thighs and paunch now turned a dirty white, whilst his pudgy face had the blackened, twisted look of a hanged man. He just sprawled, mouth gaping, eyes staring. Beside him was the bony, thin corpse of the whore; her head, face down on the dirty sheets, covered by a red wig which now hung askew, one hand across the summoner's portly chest so that even in death she seemed to want to comfort him. Colum turned her body over. The flaccid breasts bounced slightly, her arms sprawled lifeless like the wings of a dead bird. Kathryn edged closer and stared down at the painted face, the yellowing teeth framed between carmine-painted lips; her skin had the same darkish tinge as that of the summoner.

'By the stones!' Colum breathed. 'Not a pretty sight.'

'Death never is,' Kathryn replied. She heard a retching sound and turned to see Luberon standing in the corner, one hand against the wall, gagging and vomiting. 'There is no need for you to stay, Master Clerk,' she said softly. She looked at the reddish patches on both corpses. 'I think they drank enough poison to slay the entire tavern.'

Kathryn closed their eyes and eased the whore's corpse slightly to one side. She picked up the battered jug which lay between the bodies; its contents had stained the grimy sheets. She walked round the bed and found the pewter cups which had been cast there as the couple had gone into their violent death-throes. Both were empty. Kathryn sniffed each one carefully and looked at Colum.

'Never drink coarse wine,' she said. 'God knows what it can hide!'

She took the wine jar and smashed it against the wall. Then, crouching down, she sifted amongst the shards, picking up the clay base.

'Why did you do that?' Colum came and squatted beside her.

Kathryn picked up one of the rushes and carefully scraped the shattered base.

'You can see the wine,' she said. 'But notice this sludge, like the ooze of a pond?'

'Wouldn't wine leave that?' Colum asked.

Kathryn shook her head. 'No, this is soft and recent, like a thick powder. Wine silt is different, more like grains of sand.'

'So what is it?'

'As yet I'm not sure, but I have my suspicions.'

She rose and washed her hands in a bowl of water, gingerly drying them on a soiled napkin, then went with Colum out into the passageway, where a white-faced Luberon was waiting.

'You can have the corpses removed,' Kathryn said. 'Both unfortunates were murdered. Yet I doubt we'll learn much here.'

They went downstairs, where a frightened taverner told them that the summoner had arrived the previous day and spent a great deal of time in the taproom. Later that night he had been joined by the whore.

'Did they know each other?' Kathryn asked sharply.

'No, no, the woman came in, looked around and asked if there was a summoner here. She then went and joined him.'

'And the wine?' Colum asked.

The fellow pulled a face. 'The summoner drank what

we have, but the whore brought her own jug, sealed at the neck. I didn't want any trouble, so I left them alone.' He turned, hawked and spat. 'You know what these petty officials are like. Interfere with their pleasures and they are on your back for life. Now can I get on with the day's business?'

Luberon agreed and they went back into the yard, where the serjeant still stood guarding their horses. Kathryn breathed in deeply; after the tavern, even the manure piled high in the corner of the yard smelt sweet.

'You think that was the work of our murderer?' Luberon asked.

'Yes, I do,' Kathryn replied. 'And what's more, whoever killed him is a physician.'

'How so?'

'Well, the taverner said the woman arrived late. The Captain of the Guard did not allow her through Westgate, so the only way she left the city was through the postern door. All of our physician friends have a key to that.'

Colum helped her remount and smiled up at her.

'And what else, most astute of physicians?'

Kathryn gathered the reins in her hand and ignored the banter.

'I think she was hired by a physician, well paid, given that jug of poisoned wine, then sent through the postern gate to entertain the summoner.' Kathryn nodded, looking back at the tavern. 'Our noble innkeeper, whatever he may say, has been through the pockets of both victims and kept whatever monies he has found.' She looked round at Luberon. 'Who found the corpses?'

'Oh, one of the slatterns doing her morning rounds.'

'Did any of the customers know the whore?'

Luberon shrugged.

'You can always ask,' Colum hinted.

Luberon dismounted, swaggered back to the tavern and returned a few minutes later scratching his head.

'They are not sure, but they think it's Peg of Bullpaunch

Alley, one of those reeking runnels in Westgate Ward near Saint Peter's Church.'

Kathryn sighed and closed her eyes.

'Hell's kitchen,' she murmured to Colum. 'A tangle of dirty alley-ways and passages where you can hire a girl for a penny.' She looked at Luberon. 'Do any of our physician friends work there?'

Luberon smiled for the first time that day. 'Yes, three of them do. There is some charity, you know the sort. A bequest, left to the church of Saint Peter's, which pays for physicians to tend the sick and infirm in the quarter.' Luberon mounted his own cob and sat thinking to himself.

'Yes, Master Luberon?' Colum persisted.

The clerk coughed nervously. 'I don't live in Westgate,' he answered defensively. 'But, amongst my many duties, I am a warden of Saint Peter's Church, that's how I know about the charity. The parish priest there, Father Raoul, often talks about the good work the physicians do.'

'Which ones?' Kathryn asked, steadying her horse, which stirred restlessly as ostlers and stable-boys began to move round the yard.

'Well, at first it was a physician who lived there but that didn't last long, so the bequest was paid to the collegium: Darryl, Straunge and Chaddedon.'

'So,' Colum observed, 'that leaves Cotterell out!'

Luberon shook his head and urged his horse forward.

'Oh, no, it doesn't,' he breathed.

They waited until they were on the track leading down to Westgate. Colum winked at Kathryn and pushed alongside Luberon, tugging gently at the reins of his horse.

'You were going to say something else, Master Clerk?'

Luberon reined in and looked round, as if eavesdroppers lurked behind the hedges. He glanced quickly at Kathryn and licked his dry lips.

'Our fat physician . . .' he whispered. 'Well, he's a

strange man with peculiar tastes.' Luberon looked down and plucked a loose thread from his cloak.

'And he can satisfy those tastes in Westgate?' Kathryn continued.

Luberon nodded.

'And you, Master Luberon,' Colum said. 'Were you in Westgate yesterday?'

'Yes, yes, I was,' the little man answered quickly. 'I told you, I am a warden of Saint Peter's Church, though the others could also have been there.'

'Why do you say that?'

Luberon pointed at the spire of a church just jutting above the city walls. 'That's Holy Cross Church. I know they were all there yesterday with the Guild of Jesus Mass, preparing the mystery play.'

Colum followed the direction of Luberon's outstretched hand, then stared up at the sky. 'It's going to be a beautiful day,' he said. 'I have business to do.' He looked quickly at Kathryn. 'Shall we visit our doctor friends and ask them where they all were yesterday?'

'We'd hardly be welcome,' Kathryn replied. She grasped the reins of her horse more tightly. 'And I have business back at Ottemelle Lane.' She looked angrily at Luberon. 'Believe me, Sir, the city will get their pound of flesh from me.'

The clerk, still subdued after his confession, just shrugged and urged his horse forward. 'There's no need to visit their house,' he called over his shoulder. 'Mistress Swinbrooke, my belly's still empty, and our physicians will assemble early at Holy Cross Church. I suggest we eat and wait for them there.'

Colum and Kathryn agreed. They entered Westgate and consumed some oatcakes and watered ale at a tavern just within the city walls. They heard the burghmote horn sound loud and clear for the day's business in the market to begin, so they gathered their horses and rode across St Dunstan's Lane and down to the Holy Cross Church. The cemetery and churchyard off Horsemill Lane were a bustle of activity as painters and carpenters hurried in and out of the great door above which Christ, carved in stone, sat in judgement. A pompous beadle tried to stop Colum, but the Irishman just pushed him aside and walked into the darkened nave. This had been cleared of all its benches and chairs, which were stacked high in the transepts.

At the far end of the nave, just where the light poured through the great stained-glass windows above the sanctuary, a huge stage had been erected against the high carved rood-screen. Around this scurried a host of carpenters carrying wooden frames they had cut. Several painters were working on a huge piece of canvas which would serve as the scenery. Kathryn smiled as she watched this hive of activity. When she was a child her father had often brought her here to watch the play. She remembered arriving early to secure a place at the front; her father would squat, his back to one of the pillars, and she would sit on his lap and watch, open-mouthed, as the mummers and players depicted the history of salvation from Adam's fall to Christ's harrowing Hell. The huge stage would bring the Bible to life: Abraham, knife raised high, ready to offer Isaac, only to be stopped by an angel dressed in a white gown, his hair all golden; the deluge of water as Noah and his family took refuge in the Ark; the Tower of Babel; and so on. The play would last for hours, and yet she would go home disappointed it had not continued longer. Colum seized her by the elbow and pointed to a group in the far corner near a small side door.

'We have found our quarry,' he muttered and strode purposefully down the nave, leaving Kathryn and Luberon to hurry behind him.

The group turned and Kathryn recognised the physicians, all dressed soberly in dark fustian gowns covered in dust and specks of woodchip. They were conversing with the chief carpenter and their dour looks conveyed deep displeasure at seeing Kathryn and Colum so soon again.

'May I have a word?' Colum abruptly asked.

Chaddedon attempted a faint smile. Straunge exhaled heavily. Cotterell, who still looked much the worse for wear after a night of heavy drinking, just gazed blearily back. Chaddedon whispered to the chief carpenter; once the fellow was gone, Chaddedon rubbed his hands together.

'What's the matter now, Master Murtagh?'

'Another murder!' Luberon answered.

'In Christ's name!' Straunge muttered.

'Aye,' Kathryn replied. 'Christ will be concerned, as will be the King, not to mention His Grace the Archbishop.'

'His Grace is furious,' Luberon added. 'And the burgesses elected to the King's great parliament at Westminster will be carrying petitions about the loss of trade these terrible murders are causing.'

'This is no place to discuss it,' Chaddedon replied.

He led them outside, turning left along a beaten track across the cemetery, not stopping till they reached the shade of grotesquely twisted yew-trees. They stood in a semi-circle, the physicians muttering and grumbling, shifting uneasily, so the birds flew noisily from the branches above them. Colum, his thumbs through his belt, looked aggressive and bad-tempered. Kathryn sensed his deep dislike for these well-fed, pampered burgesses, who could organise a play in the nave of a church but showed little concern about the grisly murders occurring in the city. He would have lectured them all but Kathryn tactfully intervened.

'There have been two murders,' she announced, 'at the Fastolf Inn.' She graphically described the circumstances of the murders and watched the colour drain even from Cotterell's rubicund face. 'So you can see,' Kathryn concluded flatly, 'the murderer must be a physician with a ready supply of poison and a key to the postern gate.'

'But it still doesn't mean it's one of us!' Straunge spat back.

'I follow the drift of Mistress Swinbrooke's conversation,' Chaddedon replied. He looked slyly at Cotterell. 'Master Geoffrey may have to make home visits in Westgate, but so do we. A bequest given to Saint Peter's Church pays for doctors to work amongst the poor in that ward.' He looked defiantly at Murtagh. 'I worked there yesterday. I visited two sick children in a house not far from Bullpaunch Alley.'

'I was there yesterday morning,' Straunge said.

Colum looked at Darryl.

'I spent most of the day here,' the physician retorted. 'But, before you imply it, Irishman, let me speak your thoughts.' He shot a hand out. 'Holy Cross Church is only a walk away from Westgate, and yes, I could have slipped across into that maze of alleys to hire a whore and give her a poisoned jug of wine. But I didn't!'

'Everyone knew Peg,' Chaddedon intervened. 'A mean-mouthed, avaricious wench, who would seize any opportunity to insult me and my colleagues.'

'Mind you,' Cotterell interrupted spitefully, 'others could have gone there.' He looked meaningfully at Luberon.

The little clerk jumped up and down in his anger. 'I have already explained,' he repeated, 'about my post of warden at Saint Peter's Church.'

'Gentlemen! Gentlemen!' Colum laughed, now enjoying himself. 'All we came here to do was to ask questions, not make accusations.'

'No! No!' Darryl replied. 'It's the same thing, Irishman.' He stared round at his companions. 'We are innocent of these accusations.' He pulled his robe around him. 'And unless you can bring positive proof, I do not wish to be questioned further!'

He was about to stalk off when Newington hurried through the cemetery towards them. The alderman looked fresh and relaxed, and he nodded at Luberon.

'Good morning, Master Clerk. I heard the news. Another murder! Well, well, Master Murtagh,' he continued, 'a pretty mess. A pretty mess.'

'Are you alderman of that ward?' Colum accused.

Newington stepped back. 'Which one?'

'Westgate. The whore who died came from there.'

Newington threw his head back and cackled with laughter. 'Lord save us, Irishman, I would never set foot there. My ward's where my good son-in-law lives. I was born and raised there. No, no,' he breathed. 'If I had my way, I'd burn Westgate to the ground!'

Kathryn looked at Colum. 'There's little more we can do,' she said. 'And Master Darryl's right. Unless we can produce proof, there is little point in having these conversations.' She glanced round at the physicians. 'Gentlemen, I bid you adieu.' And before Colum could stop her, she walked across the cemetery back towards the main gate of the church.

'You were too easy on them!'

She stopped and turned; Colum stood glaring at her. Kathryn leaned against the wall of the church. She watched two lads carrying a pile of costumes, dresses, shawls, wings for an angel, a silver moon and a golden sun into the church.

'What can we do?' she sighed. 'This murderer has every advantage.'

'We could go to Westgate,' Luberon squeaked, coming up huffing and puffing up beside them. 'We could at least make enquiries there.'

'Aye, and at Saint Peter's Church,' Kathryn mused. 'Something's wrong . . .' Her voice trailed off. She was determined to go to Westgate, but did not wish to arouse anyone's suspicions.

Colum tightened his sword-belt. 'Sufficient unto the day is the evil thereof,' he quipped, and winked at Luberon. 'Yes, Master Clerk, I know some Scripture. Mistress Kathryn, I do have other duties to carry out.'

'Haven't we all?' Kathryn retorted.

Colum just pulled a face and walked out of the church into the crowds milling about outside. Kathryn watched him go, then glanced at Luberon.

'Well, Master Clerk, shall we test our fortune in Westgate?'

Luberon looked at the sun now high in the sky. 'I'll go with you, Mistress. You can't go there by yourself, but first, I need to see John.'

'Who?'

'Newington,' Luberon exclaimed. 'John Newington. I must discuss this business with him. Would you wait?'

Kathryn nodded and sauntered out of the church gate. The good weather had brought the crowds into Horsemill Lane. They were now packed around the stalls set up under the eaves of the houses opposite the church. Most of the merchandise was cloth, green tartan cushions with silk borders, scarlet gowns with damask sleeves, colourful arras, silken testers, counterpanes, sheets and napery. Kathryn looked at these, keeping a hand on her purse as she caught sight of Rathead, a small greasy-haired urchin who lived with his mother in an alley-way off Ottemelle Lane. Rathead had fingers nimbler than any seamstress and was gaining a growing reputation as a sharp foist or pickpocket.

Kathryn moved farther down the street. Knowing Luberon would be some time, she stopped to gaze at other stalls selling saucers, dishes, paternosters, amber beads and pewter cups. She heard a commotion behind her, and looking back at the street saw a small crowd gathering round the battered market cross where a pardoner had set up a stall. The man had the face of a bird, a high-beaked nose and large protuberant eyes; his neck, scrawny with muscle, reminded Kathryn of an angry chicken in a farmyard.

'Good citizens!' the pardoner shouted. 'I can show you the comb of the cock that crowed in Pilate's courtyard, a splinter from Noah's great Ark and, look'—he held up a quill—'a feather from one of God's own angels!'

'More likely from the goose you ate for dinner yesterday!' someone shouted back.

Kathryn smiled and watched the pardoner return the good-natured abuse. She remembered Chaucer's *Canterbury Tales* and what she had discovered the previous evening. She pushed her way through the crowd, walked back into the churchyard and sat on a stone bench outside the main door. She knew she had met the murderer, but how could she prove it? How could she stop the assassin from killing again? She watched a child playing in the street.

'Mistress! Mistress!'

She looked up. Luberon, his pompous face red and sweaty, peered down at her.

'Mistress, there is still so much to do.'

'Aye, Master Luberon, then it's best we do it!'

Chapter 11

Kathryn and Luberon walked up past Westgate into Pound Lane. The streets and alley-ways became more tangled, dirty and darker. The houses had seen better days and their crumbling plaster was now dirty grey and moist. On the street corners stood a shifty collection of labourers, beggars, touts and broken servants. Kathryn glimpsed angry eyes in baleful faces and she was sure that some in the crowd would have accosted her if it had not been for Luberon swaggering along beside her. The clerk might be pompous, but he had all the courage of a fighting cock. He stuck out his little chest and had pulled back his cloak to reveal the long stabbing dagger tucked into his belt.

'Men at war with the law,' he murmured, gazing round.

They went deeper into the slums. Some of the alleyways were so dark, lanterns had been lit and slung on hooks outside the doors. Luberon explained how beneath these houses were cellars where the topers could rest at night.

'They have hangers,' he explained, 'ropes tied from one wall to the other so the topers can sleep sitting up, with the upper part of their bodies supported by these cords.

In the morning the landlord comes down and rudely awakens them by loosening the ropes.'

At last they reached Bullpaunch Alley. The Rat's Castle Tavern stood on the corner, and outside it withered children, little more than living skeletons, danced to the reedy tune of a pipe. Kathryn's hand went to draw pennies from her purse.

'No, no!' Luberon whispered. 'No charity, Mistress. If they see your coins, it will only whet their appetites.'

They went deeper into the alley-way. Women, their faces dirty and greasy, stood behind small stalls and sold the flesh of rats, ferrets and pigeons, as well as the skins of cats. Luberon stopped and asked one of these a question. The woman replied with a hurl of abuse and pointed farther down the street. Luberon walked on and knocked on the decaying door of the house she had indicated.

An old beldame, a veritable night-bird hag, answered. Her face was gaunt and yellowing, grey wispy hair straggled down to her shoulders; she had thin, bloodless lips and eyes which looked a thousand years old. She glanced at Luberon, then at Kathryn.

'Well, well, a man and his doxy.' She looked slyly at Kathryn. 'I have never seen you before. You look the stern type. Have you a riding crop?'

Luberon went puce-faced and speechless. Kathryn just stared at this hag, who thought she was Luberon's mistress, and burst into peals of laughter. The old night-bird, realising her mistake, went to close the door, but Luberon recovered his wits and kicked it back on its hinges.

'You stupid bitch!' he roared. 'I am a city official!'

The old woman, her eyes now fearful, stepped back into the shadows, her lips parted in an ingratiating smirk.

'What is it?' she whimpered. 'What do you want?'

Luberon and Kathryn followed her down a dank passageway. Kathryn was still giggling to herself, but Luberon was so outraged he pushed the woman farther down into the house until she stopped, her back against a door.

'Aren't you going to invite us in?' Luberon snarled.

The hag was about to object but Luberon's hand went to his dagger, so she nervously felt for the handle, pushed it down and beckoned them on. Inside, the room was surprisingly opulent, even rich, but everything was of black accented with gold. The hangings on the wall, the woollen rugs on the floor, the high carved mantelpiece; even the tables, chairs, chests and stools had been painted a glossy black which caught and reflected the light of the fire burning in the grate. Two oil-lamps glowed dimly against the wall on either side of the fireplace; at Luberon's bidding, the woman hastily lighted some candles, their wax also dyed black. Kathryn looked down at the floor and the smile died on her lips. The rugs were covered in strange signs, inverted crosses, a pentacle, whilst on the wall farther down the room an artist had depicted a grinning skeleton, arms extended.

'Well! Well!' Luberon murmured, looking round, 'What do we have here? A mistress of the black arts? A witch?' He gave the old hag a slight push. 'Or just a well-paid keeper of perfumed flesh?'

'The room was like this when I bought it,' the old woman whined.

'Oh, we are not here for your bloody room!' Luberon snapped. He jabbed a finger at the ceiling. 'One of your customers. I think she had a garret here?'

'Which one?' the hag replied.

'Peg.'

'You mean Mustard Peg?' The old woman cackled. 'Hot to the touch she is!'

Kathryn stared at her in disgust. She realised how cold the room was and flinched at the sweet sickly smell which now cloyed her nose and mouth.

'Peg's been murdered,' Kathryn announced abruptly.

The old woman made a face. 'So?'

'So,' Luberon continued, going over to the fireplace and plucking a brand out of the flames. 'Unless you tell us who came here to hire her yesterday, I'll drop this on the rug and watch this bloody house burn.'

'You wouldn't dare!'

Luberon threw the firebrand back and wiped dirty fingers on his gown. 'No, perhaps I wouldn't. But I could bring soldiers and officials to search here. Who knows what they might find?'

'What do you want to know?'

The old hag drew closer and Kathryn wrinkled her nose at the sour smell from her body.

'Peg was hired yesterday,' Kathryn replied. 'You know who visited her?'

'Don't lie!' Luberon added.

The old woman bared her gums. 'Why should I lie? There's not much to say. Yesterday afternoon Peg had a visitor. He came here in the afternoon, when she was resting between her labours. He spoke to her for a while, then left. Peg seemed happy enough but would not say who it was or what he wanted.' The old woman looked slyly at Kathryn. 'You know the way of the world, Mistress. We have many visitors here.'

'Then what?' Kathryn asked.

'Late in the evening Peg left.' The hag shrugged. 'She was a loud-mouthed bitch and probably got what she deserved.'

'Did you see the visitor in the afternoon?' Kathryn asked.

'Oh, no, he was cowled and hooded like a monk. If that's the way they like it, that's the way I take it.' The old woman peered at Kathryn. 'You're very pretty, Mistress.'

'Come on!' Luberon growled, plucking at Kathryn's sleeve. 'This place stinks like a sewer!'

'Peg had a room here?' Kathryn asked.

The hag nodded and grinned. 'It's empty. If any of the girls is late, I always have a look around.'

'I am sure you do,' Luberon jibed.

He told Kathryn to wait and prodded the old woman up the shabby stairs. He came clattering down sooner than she expected, a look of disgust on his face.

'A pigpen,' he murmured. 'Shared with others. A battered cup and some tawdry linen. Mustard Peg died penniless.'

They left the dreadful house in Bullpaunch Alley, threading their way through the lanes until they reached St Peter's Lane.

'Well,' Kathryn began, 'what do you make of all that, Master Clerk?'

Luberon looked at the houses on either side of them, which were better-kept, and the lane leading down to the church was broader and cleaner, a welcome contrast to the runnels they had just been through.

'I don't know,' Luberon mumbled. 'We learnt very little.'

'Yes, we did,' Kathryn replied briskly. 'Our murderer apparently visited that house early yesterday afternoon, paid for Peg's services and told her to meet him at a certain hour near one of the postern gates.' She plucked the kerchief from her sleeve and dabbed at the sweat forming on her brow. 'But I agree, that tells us nothing new. Any of those physicians could have slipped out of Holy Cross Church and done all that before returning home.'

Kathryn stared down at the turreted tower of St Peter's, recalling what she had read in Chaucer's *Canterbury Tales* and the vague ideas which had occurred to her outside Holy Cross Church. She just wished Colum were there. Kathryn clenched her fist; Colum was supposed to be the King's bloody Commissioner here, and she, too, had other business to attend to. Suddenly she thought of her husband, his long pale face changed to a mask of fury after several cups of wine. Kathryn closed her eyes. She must not think of him, of the possibilities surrounding his mysterious disappearance.

'Mistress! Mistress!'

Kathryn opened her eyes and stared at Luberon.

'Mistress Swinbrooke, you wish to visit Saint Peter's Church?'

'Will the priest assist us?'

'It depends on what you are going to ask.'

Kathryn grinned. 'Come along and discover for yourself.'

They found Father Raoul busily hoeing a large garden patch which stretched between the church and the priest's house. He was a square, thick-set man, with the broad face of a farmer and tousled brown hair which looked as if it hadn't been combed for a month. Yet he was cheerful and friendly, and he warmly welcomed Luberon, though he was rather shy of Kathryn.

'I am only too glad for a rest,' the priest exclaimed, dropping the hoe and wiping soiled hands on his gown. 'Come into the house.'

He led them into the kitchen, a stark room with an earth-beaten floor, lime-washed walls and a few sticks of furniture. He invited them to sit at the small trestle-table and served stoups of cold ale, tangy and sweet to the taste.

'Well,' he said, smacking his lips, 'what can I do for you?'

Luberon continued the introductions he had made in the garden, spoke briefly about the murders, then coughed and looked at Kathryn.

'Father, you knew Peg of Bullpaunch Alley?' she asked.

Father Raoul smiled. 'Not in the biblical sense. Peg was a fearsome woman, God rest her.'

'How many years have you been here, Father?'

'About fifteen summers. Why?'

'You were—or rather, the church here—was left a bequest to hire doctors who would work amongst the poor?'

Father Raoul shrugged. 'That's quite common. Churches up and down the kingdom are endowed with legacies or sums of money. Such sums, usually deposited with bankers, are drawn on according to the needs of the parish. The accounts are scrutinised and checked by good men like Master Luberon.'

'Who gave this bequest?'

The priest sighed, then rose and went across to a huge chest against the far wall. He took a bunch of keys from his belt and carefully unlocked the three clasps, rummaged inside and brought out a leather-bound ledger; the parchment inside was yellow and greasy with age. Father Raoul peered down the pages, muttering to himself, then stopped and stabbed an entry with his finger. He turned the ledger round so Kathryn could inspect it.

'The bequest is some eighteen years old. A generous amount. Three hundred pounds sterling, but, like many bequests, it was anonymous.'

'And you have no idea who was the donor?'

'No, and I suspect the bankers themselves do not know. Such monies are given and held in trust.' Father Raoul shrugged and closed the book.

Kathryn bit back her disappointment. 'Do the names Darryl, Cotterell, Straunge and Chaddedon mean anything to you?'

'Well, Cotterell I have seen in the alleys and streets around the Rat's Castle Tavern. He skulks there to buy his pleasures.' The contempt in the priest's voice was obvious.

'And the others?'

Father Raoul waved his hand at Luberon. 'As our good clerk knows, they do some good work amongst the poor, like other merchants, tailors, tradesmen and burgesses. They visit the sick and do what they can, which usually isn't much, and every quarter present their bill.'

'And Newington?' Kathryn asked. 'John Newington the alderman?'

Father Raoul pursed his lips and shook his head. 'I have heard the name but never met him. He has little to do with this quarter of the city.'

Kathryn sat, hands in her lap. Nothing, she thought; everywhere I turn there is a dead end. She must have sat for at least five minutes, lost in her own thoughts, whilst Luberon and Father Raoul discussed parish matters.

'Mistress Swinbrooke,' Father Raoul said, 'is there anything else you wish to know?'

Kathryn glared in exasperation at the ledger.

'Your parish serves this ward?'

'Of course.'

'Father, has anything happened? Anything at all in the last year which you thought untoward or rather strange?'

'Such as?'

Kathryn closed her eyes and thought of the assassin. He killed for a motive, he hated the shrine. He had the resources and wealth to move secretly round the city. She remembered "The Knight's Tale" in Chaucer's collection.

'Mistress Swinbrooke,' Father Raoul repeated rather testily, 'such as what?'

'A funeral, a death?'

Father Raoul sat back and laughed. 'Thanks to the sweating sickness, there have been many of those.'

'No.' Kathryn leaned across the table. 'Has there been a death, a funeral, which perhaps didn't fit in with the usual routine of your parish?' Her eyes bored into Raoul. 'You know, Father, someone whose death was unexpected or unexplained? Or a funeral shrouded in mystery?'

Father Raoul shook his head. 'Mistress Swinbrooke, you have seen my parish. When my people go into God's acre they are covered in a canvas sheet and shoved into a shallow hole. I bless the corpse and sing a Mass and'—his voice broke off. 'Except . . .'

'Except what, Father?'

'Except this past March, just before Lady Day. An old woman died, yes, Christina Oldstrom. She was a seamstress who lived down an alley-way just off Pound Lane.' The priest fingered his lips. 'Christina was a strange woman,' he continued. 'They say she was of a good family but she fell on hard times. She kept to herself.'

'Did she have any kin?'

'Not that I know of. But it was strange.' Father Raoul held his hand up. 'Oh, she was pious and devout, but on the few occasions I visited her house, though the outside was shabby, inside she never lacked for comfort. Enough coal and wood in winter, a proper bed, a buttery with good food and drink, and she always paid her tithes. Well, last winter, she fell ill of a wasting sickness and I directed those doctors you have mentioned to visit her, but it was fruitless. She had some terrible tumour inside which ate away her flesh.'

'Did anyone else visit her, apart from the doctors?' Luberon asked sharply.

'No, no. I always thought there was someone, but she never said anything about her past, even though she lived in comfort, well above that of a common seamstress.' Father Raoul shrugged. 'It was her business, so I never asked. Anyway, she died. She left a small will saying her chamber and all its contents were to be sold and the proceeds given to the poor.' Father Raoul looked at Luberon. 'You must remember it, Luberon. You took care of the monies. Widows and maids often make such bequests.' Father Raoul drummed his fingers on the table. 'But what was odd was that when her body was brought into church, I received silver pieces and written instructions to furnish her with a proper pine-wood coffin, have three Masses sung for her soul and a proper cross placed above her grave in the cemetery.'

'Do you still have this message?'

'No, he doesn't,' Luberon interrupted drily. 'The silver pieces were spent, the Masses sung, the coffin bought and the carpenter hired to fashion the cross.' Luberon looked away and cleared his throat. 'Women like Christina are common: lonely, poor, neglected and ill.'

'You never knew her?'

'No, of course not.'

'Come,' Father Raoul said. 'I'll show you the grave.'

He led them back into the sunshine and round the church to the broad, clean-kept cemetery. They wound their way along the paths between the headstones and graves. At last Father Raoul stopped before one. The earth was now flattened, the flowers placed there rotting and decayed, but the cross, though weather-beaten, still sturdily held its place. Kathryn peered closer and read the inscribed words: 'Christina Oldstrom. *Requiescat in Pace,* May she rest in peace.' She stared at Raoul.

'And no one came forward to claim the corpse? Or declare themselves a relative?'

Father Raoul shook his head.

'And this mysterious donor?'

'Mistress Swinbrooke,' the priest pleaded. 'Such anonymous donations are common. All I remember is the purse being handed in. I carried out my duties and reported what had happened to the parish council.'

'Father, do you know anything else about Christina Oldstrom?'

'I have told you all. She was a seamstress of some sixty years or more.'

'But she must have had another life?' Kathryn persisted. 'There must be other entries? Did she ever marry? Did she have children?'

Father Raoul breathed in deeply, looked up and watched the larks spinning against the blue sky. 'I shouldn't do this,' he murmured. 'But you may look at the parish records; births, deaths and marriages.'

'Is that necessary?' Luberon shifted uneasily. 'What are you looking for, Mistress?'

'I don't know,' Kathryn declared. 'But you, Master Clerk, can help me.'

Father Raoul was most helpful and, aided by a reluctant Luberon, Kathryn began to go through dusty old ledgers and greasy rolls of parchment, scrutinising the entries very carefully for Christina Oldstrom's name. An hour passed. At last Luberon's exasperation spilt over and, claiming he had other things to do, he stalked out of the priest's house. Father Raoul went back to his garden, now and again returning to enquire if Kathryn needed a cup of water or some more ale. Kathryn, not even bothering to look up, just shook her head and continued her study of the different scrawling handwritings of the parish priests of St Peter's. At last she discovered Christina Oldstrom's own baptismal entry for 1410, during the reign of Henry IV. She was about to turn the page when her eye caught another entry. *"Filius natus Christina Oldstrom,* a son born to Christina Oldstrom." She stopped and studied the words carefully, memorising the date, before moving the pages quickly forward, but there was nothing else to be discovered. Kathryn closed the book, rose and went out into the garden.

'Are you finished, Mistress Swinbrooke?' Father Raoul called.

'Yes, yes, I am,' Kathryn replied absent-mindedly.

'Mistress, is there anything wrong?'

'No, no. I must buy some sweetmeats.'

And, watched by a mystified priest, Kathryn walked down the path to the lych-gate.

Thomasina had also been busy that morning. There had been a few callers: a child with a scalded hand; Beeton the brewer, complaining of his gout; a young man with a sore gum who begged for some oil of cloves. Thomasina dealt with them all, cleared the kitchen table, gave Agnes her orders and, collecting her cloak, left the house and went purposefully up Ottemelle Lane and down Hethenman Lane towards St Mildred's Church. She entered its dark coolness and stood near the baptismal font next to the door. Members of the parish council were moving about at the top of the nave, preparing the altar for the Feast of the Precious Blood. Some were polishing the rood-screen, others trimming candles or carrying cushions and testers into the sanctuary. Thomasina stood and watched for a while. She glimpsed her quarry but waited until these self-important members of the parish council had left to return to their homes.

After a while some of the group, shouting farewells, made their way down the nave, led by Joscelyn, the kinsman of Kathryn. Beside him stalked his thin, vinegarish wife whom Thomasina secretly considered to be one of the greatest shrews she had ever met. Joscelyn saw Thomasina and came towards her, scratching his balding pate as if embarrassed by the meeting.

'Thomasina.' The watery eyes narrowed in a false smile. 'And how is Mistress Kathryn?'

'She could be dead, for all your concern!' Thomasina snapped.

Again the false smile.

'Will she open the shop to sell herbs and spices?'

Thomasina noticed the greed in Joscelyn's eyes. 'Oh, yes,' she lied, 'she intends opening very soon.' She saw with satisfaction the concern in Joscelyn's face. 'Of course, Master Joscelyn,' Thomasina mockingly gasped, 'that may well affect your trade!'

Joscelyn, a spicer by trade, drew his head back like an angry duck. 'But she has no licence from the Guild!' he snorted. 'No licence from the Guild! That is not right!' And shaking his head, he rejoined his wife and stalked out of the church.

Thomasina stuck her tongue out at his retreating back and went up the nave, under the large rood-screen and into the sanctuary. Only one person remained, standing at the top of the altar steps with her back to Thomasina.

'Widow Gumple,' Thomasina whispered. 'Are we alone?'

Gumple whirled round, her white dumpling face looking slightly ridiculous under its ornate head-dress. Thomasina moved slowly towards her.

'Are we alone, Widow Gumple?' she repeated.

Widow Gumple licked her lips nervously. 'Why, yes, Thomasina,' she replied. 'They have all gone. Father has taken the viaticum to a sick parishioner.'

'Good.' Thomasina pointed to the sacristy door. 'What I have to say to you is best said in the utmost privacy.'

'Oh, don't be silly!' Gumple said, recovering her poise. 'What could you have to say to me?'

Thomasina drew herself up to her full height and pointed dramatically at the widow.

'Mistress Gumple!' she bawled, her voice echoing like a bell round the church. 'I accuse you, before God and man, of being a blackmailer!'

Gumple's jaw sagged. 'What do you mean?' she whispered.

'What I say,' Thomasina replied.

Gumple's eyes fell away; she lifted the hem of her gown and walked daintily down the steps.

'Perhaps it's best,' she hissed, 'if we did talk.'

She had hardly reached the bottom step when Thomasina gave her a great push, sending Widow Gumple across the sanctuary and through the half-open sacristy door. Thomasina followed like a mastiff closing in for the kill. Gumple now looked terrified. Her head-dress slipping down over her eyes, she was backed against the wall.

'Sit down!' Thomasina ordered.

Gumple crouched on the stool pushed towards her. Thomasina towered over her, thrusting a clenched fist close to Gumple's fleshy nose.

'I don't like you, Widow Gumple!' Thomasina told her. 'You are a hypocrite, and you spend most of your time around this church snatching every bit of tawdry glory you can, but that's your business. As it is also your business if you have a liking for young men and pay for their favours!'

Gumple just stared back, her eyes like little black currants, terrified by the fury towering over her.

'Young men like Alexander Wyville,' Thomasina continued. 'I suspect you knew him before his marriage to my mistress. God only knows whether, even after vows were exchanged, you continued your relationship with him!'

Gumple's mouth opened and closed.

'Don't explain to me,' Thomasina said. 'Your life is your own, but what do you know about Alexander Wyville's disappearance? And why did you send that note to my mistress, demanding gold be left on a gravestone in the cemetery?'

'I sent no note,' Gumple bleated.

'Yes, you did, but my mistress never received it. I did. I went to the cemetery and hid there. Apart from two lovers who would not know Alexander from Adam, the only person who came into that graveyard was you!' Thomasina crouched over her. 'Oh, you opened the side door and looked out as if concerned about some parish matter, but what were you really looking for? My mistress? Or the gold she might bring? Or were you just trying to trap her into making some admission?'

Widow Gumple shook her head wordlessly.

'You snivelling tub of lard!' Thomasina growled. 'I admit, physician Swinbrooke did a terrible thing. He tried to poison the man who was beating his daughter. But when he returned to his house, he found Alexander gone and the only trace was Wyville's cloak, left near his favourite spot by the riverside. I think you know the place well, you must have met Alexander there on a number of occasions.' Thomasina cleared her throat. 'Now, I suspect this is what happened: Alexander Wyville drank the poisoned wine, but he was so deep in his cups he must have retched and vomited most of it. Nevertheless, he knew something was wrong. He staggered out of the gate at the back of physician Swinbrooke's house and into the alleyway. He either went to you or you met him. Perhaps you helped clean his belly of everything he had drunk. Anyway, Wyville had no desire to return and confront physician Swinbrooke, so he left his cloak by the river bank and, assisted by you, snuck out of the city to join Faunte and the other rebels.' Thomasina pushed her face only inches away from Widow Gumple. 'I am right, aren't I?' she accused. 'And don't lie! Do you know the punishment for blackmail? To be burned alive in a barrel of oil, that is if I don't kill you first!' Thomasina put her hand beneath her cloak as if searching for a dagger. 'But if you confess the truth,' she continued sweetly, 'then it will be our secret. I swear by the cross I will not tell Mistress Swinbrooke. Though, of course, those letters must stop.'

Gumple, witless with terror, nodded her head.

'Well?'

'I knew Alexander Wyville,' Gumple began hesitantly. 'He was a member of this parish. I used to . . . well . . . talk to him. I . . .' she stammered, 'I was surprised when he became the betrothed of Mistress Swinbrooke because I knew something of his little ways, his love of wine, his violent temper. Anyway'—she put her head-dress straight—'the marriage took place.' Gumple paused and stared out of the door.

Aye, Thomasina thought, and I'll wager you laughed secretly at the pig in the poke the Swinbrookes had taken into their house. 'Go on!' she ordered loudly.

'Well, Alexander told me he was leaving to join the Lancastrian army. He said he loved Kathryn but he found her cold, ice-like and distant, whilst he was in awe of her father. One night he came to my house in a terrible state; his doublet was stained with wine and he stank like a pig. He claimed he had been poisoned by physician Swinbrooke and only saved himself through vomiting. Nevertheless, he complained of pains in his belly. I stuck a goose quill down his throat and made him sick even further, then I made him drink jug after jug of water. After that he slept for a while. When he awoke, he was still terrified that Swinbrooke would search him out and kill him. I asked him why and he confessed to the terrible beatings he had given Kathryn. Wyville said he wanted to leave his marriage, he was tired of Canterbury and he would seek his fortune with the Lancastrians. His purse was full of silver. I gave him some of my late husband's clothes. Wyville told me to leave his own cloak on the river bank in the hope the Swinbrookes might think he had drowned. That is the last I ever saw of him.'

'You are sure?'

Widow Gumple struggled to her feet. 'I swear!' she said. 'I swear!'

'And the letters you sent to Mistress Kathryn?'

'I have never liked physician Swinbrooke, and his daughter is so full of airs and graces . . .' Gumple shrugged at Thomasina's fierce gaze. 'I thought she had betrothed Alexander to spite me. Oh, I know Wyville did her wrong but, I thought, why should she be so serene and calm?'

'She wasn't serene and calm,' Thomasina snarled. 'Wyvillle's beatings shocked her whilst her own father eventually confessed to the terrible deed he tried to commit. My mistress was totally innocent of any wrongdoing. You had no right to hound her the way you did.' Thomasina stepped back and pointed her finger at Widow Gumple. 'I will keep your secret, but if you ever try anything like that again, I swear I will kill you!'

Chapter 12

When Thomasina arrived back in Ottemelle Lane she found Kathryn in her chamber, staring down at the Chaucer manuscript.

'Mistress?'

Kathryn turned and Thomasina was shocked by her mistress's drawn face.

'Kathryn,' she whispered. 'In God's name, what is wrong?'

Kathryn just shook her head. 'I have been to Westgate,' she replied softly. 'I went to a terrible house, then to Saint Peter's Church. After that I visited Darryl's house, but only spoke to the children.'

'And what happened?'

Kathryn refused to answer but kept her gaze on the manuscript, so Thomasina went to the buttery where Agnes was salting some meat.

'Mistress Kathryn is acting strangely,' Agnes murmured. 'She has only recently returned, white as a ghost. I told her about the message.'

Thomasina's heart skipped a beat. 'What message?'

'Oh, from the Irishman. He wants her to go out to Kingsmead, but she is in no fit state.'

'Nothing some wine mixed with herbs won't cure,' Thomasina answered, busily getting down two cups and a jug of wine. With the cups filled she went back to Kathryn, who still sat reading Chaucer's work. 'Drink, Mistress.'

Kathryn took the cup and sipped it gently. 'Not too much on an empty stomach.'

'Is it Wyville?' Thomasina asked. 'Are you still worried about what happened to him?'

Kathryn shook her head.

'No, my feelings about him are numb. God forgive me, I couldn't care if he lives or dies!'

'You realise he could still be alive?'

'Alexander Wyville's no longer my husband. If he returns, I will seek an annullment in the Church courts.'

Thomasina pulled across a stool and sat next to her mistress. 'There will be no more letters, Kathryn.'

'What do you mean?'

Thomasina smiled. 'Trust me. The letters will cease.'

Thomasina was about to question Kathryn on Colum's message from Kingsmead when there was a thunderous knocking on the door, followed by Agnes's hurried footsteps and a man's voice demanding entrance.

'It's that bloody Irishman,' Thomasina muttered.

But when she and Kathryn went into the kitchen, a sweaty red-faced Luberon stood there, holding a piece of parchment.

'Master Clerk, what is it now?'

'What is it now? What is it now?' Luberon squeaked. 'Another damn message pinned to the cathedral door. Read it!'

Kathryn took the yellowing piece of paper.

A yeoman green to Canterbury did go, alas
And I to Satan his soul did pass.

'What does he mean?' Luberon snapped. 'Who's the yeoman green?'

Kathryn studied the greasy piece of parchment and the scrawled blue ink. 'God knows,' she muttered, 'what's happening in that madman's mind!'

'Doesn't anyone see him?' Thomasina asked. 'Surely someone would notice a person pinning a piece of parchment to the cathedral door?'

'There are at least four entrances to the cathedral,' Luberon said. 'And, once inside, even more doors. A stream of pilgrims, hundreds a day, go through them there, and how long would it take? All the assassin has to do is brush by, pin up his notice and disappear into the crowd.'

'I'm only trying to help,' Thomasina retorted.

Luberon glared at her. 'God knows what we are supposed to do,' he snarled. 'Warn every knight in Canterbury? Turn back any lord from the city gates? That would cause a stir.' He blew his lips out. 'Mistress Swinbrooke, I've told you what I know.' He peered at Kathryn. 'Did you find anything at Saint Peter's?'

Kathryn looked at him strangely. 'No. No,' she lied. 'Not really.'

'Then, Mistress, I bid you adieu.' And, puffing and bustling, Luberon left the house, promising he would return the following day.

Kathryn went back to her writing-chamber whilst Thomasina loudly berated Agnes for standing about open-mouthed, listening to matters which did not concern her. Kathryn sat for a while. When Thomasina returned she firmly asked to be left alone. She did not want to reveal to anyone that she knew the identity of the killer. So far she had little proof, so how could she trap him? Kathryn stared at the grimy piece of parchment and studied the message. What did it mean: "the yeoman green"? Perhaps Colum would know. Kathryn suddenly sat up straight. Of course, that's why the message had been issued. Colum was a yeoman, a member of the royal household, and the green referred to his Irish origins. The yeoman was also described by Chaucer as "clad in hood and cloak of green."

What if the killer had struck already? The Irishman had sent a message telling her to come to Kingsmead. Had something happened? Kathryn rose to her feet.

'Thomasina, Thomasina, my cloak, quickly!' Kathryn hurried into the kitchen. 'Agnes, has any gift been left here? Sweetmeats? A bottle of wine?'

'No, Mistress.'

Thomasina came bustling back with her cloak. Kathryn ignored her furious spate of questions. Colum, she thought, had said he would be leaving Kingsmead to collect fodder for the stables, so the assassin would not know that he was lodging with her. But what would happen if Colum returned to Kingsmead and found a poisoned bottle of wine, a tray of sweetmeats or some bread and cheese left there as a gift? She breathed in deeply to stop her racing heart. God knows the assassin was cunning enough to leave some note saying it was from her or, indeed, any wellwisher in Canterbury.

'Mistress,' Thomasina pleaded, 'what is wrong?'

Kathryn stared at her. She fleetingly wondered why Thomasina was so certain those terrible messages would stop, but that would have to wait. 'Thomasina,' she insisted. 'I must go to Kingsmead! No!' Kathryn held her hand up. 'You must stay here. Allow no one in. Accept no gifts or presents. Promise me!'

Thomasina promised, but her mistress was already hurrying through the door.

Kathryn collected her gentle cob from the tavern, saddled it and went up towards Westgate. She stopped at the camp to see if she could see Colum amongst the soldiers milling about there, but all she did was attract unwanted attention, so she urged her horse on. She passed through Northgate, kept away from the city walls, following the white dusty track over the brow of a hill, not reining in until she saw the old manor and broken fences of Kingsmead. She followed the winding track down. An urchin, probably one of the soldiers' boys, sat sleeping outside the broken gate. Kathryn dismounted and shook him awake.

'Lad, is anyone here?'

'No, Mistress.' The boy's dark round eyes in his pallid face searched anxiously about. 'Why should there be? Master Murtagh and the others have left for Maidstone and the women are back at the camp.'

'And no one has come here?'

'Honestly, Mistress, who would want to come here? The place is deserted.'

'No strangers called with wine or food?'

The boy crossed his arms defensively. 'Of course not, I said so!'

Kathryn gently stroked his head. 'Then stay there, lad. When the Irishman comes, tell him Mistress Swinbrooke—you have my name?—Mistress Swinbrooke is here.'

She went through the gate and up the small path which led to the side of the manor-house. Looking round, Kathryn knew Colum could never have stayed here. The gardens were over-grown, the gulleys choked with weeds, the small fortified manor-house decaying and derelict. There were no shutters at the windows, some doors hung askew, whilst great holes gaped in the red-tiled roof, leaving the timbers beneath open to the sky. Kathryn went round to the back of the manor and found even worse: the great yard was choked with weeds, the stables, smithies and outhouses no more than ruins.

'Is there anyone here?' she called.

Not a sound. Kathryn dismounted. Colum would be here soon, perhaps he had sent the messenger on. She hobbled her horse and pushed open the small door leading into the kitchen. Inside, there was decay: the plaster on the walls was wet and rotting and Kathryn had to lift her skirts to avoid the stagnant pools of water. She went along the corridor, dark, dank and musty. The chambers on the ground floor were in total disrepair, though the stairs leading to the rooms above were made of stone and still looked safe and secure. A bird nestling in the timbers of the roof noisily flew out. Kathryn jumped and cursed her own lack of courage.

'It will take months,' she muttered to herself, 'to put this right.'

In the trees surrounding the house she heard the soft cooing of wood doves. She stood straining her ears for any sound and shivered at the awful loneliness of the place.

Kathryn suddenly froze as she heard a sound from the floor above. Was there someone there? Perhaps the messenger Colum had sent? Then she heard a groan, as if someone was in pain. She climbed half-way up the stairs.

'What is it?' she called. 'Who's there?'

Again the groan, followed by a hoarse gasp.

'Kathryn, please!'

'Colum?' she whispered.

Had Colum returned? Had something happened? She ran up the remaining steps. The door at the top was slightly ajar and she pushed it open and stepped into the gloomy chamber. The place now smelt musty and fetid; the light was poor because the only window faced east, away from the late-afternoon sun. She peered through the gloom and glimpsed the shapeless mound on the small trestle-bed in the corner.

'Colum?' she called and, taking her courage in her hands, she walked across the floor. Suddenly, one of the boards beneath her gave way, cracking and splintering. Kathryn cursed and stared up at the ceiling. Through the many holes she could see the rafters and touches of blue sky. Kathryn gingerly made her way to the bed and pulled back the blankets. At first she couldn't see; she touched the mattress beneath and felt a sticky wet ooze. As her eyes became accustomed to the gloom, she realised that the shape was no more than a bundle of rags, but at the top, where the bolster should have been, lay the decapitated head of a dog, its jaws still curled in a death-smile, its thick red tongue jutting between yellowing teeth. Kathryn screamed in horror. The door behind her slammed shut. She whirled round as a tinder flickered and the thick tallow candles on the table in the far corner flared into life.

'Who's there?' she rasped.

A shadow moved into the pool of light thrown by the candles, and Kathryn knew. 'You murdering bastard!' she hissed. She looked at the floor-boards and saw how rotten and mildewed they were. She took one step forward.

'That's far enough, bitch!' The voice was muffled and thick.

Kathryn watched as the figure stepped closer, hooded and masked, the cowl brought far across the head.

'Good day, Mistress Swinbrooke.'

Kathryn edged nearer. Suddenly the shadow moved his cloak. Kathryn heard a small click and a crossbow bolt whirled above her head and smacked into the wall behind her.

'I told you to come no nearer! I have something special for you!'

Kathryn stared at the black leather mask, but all she could see was the glint of malice behind the eye-slits.

'Why the dog?' she asked.

'A nice little touch. When I came back here the cur came snarling out, so I stabbed it and hacked the head off.'

'Where is Colum?'

'Oh, it's Colum, is it? The bastard Irishman? In Hell, for all I care!' The figure sniggered. 'He soon will be, and you can be there to welcome him!'

Kathryn wiped her sweat-soaked hands against her robe. She looked at the table beyond and glimpsed the three pewter cups.

'What is it you want?' she said, forcing her voice to remain firm.

'Your death.'

'Why?'

'Why not?'

Kathryn forced a smile. 'Well, of course you do. You love the game, don't you? Blind-man's bluff in the streets and alley-ways of Canterbury. Of course you have got to kill me. So why not stop this mummery and take your mask off? Every one will soon know, as I do, that you are Alderman John Newington!'

Again the snigger. 'But you have told no one, Kathryn, and even if you have, what proof do you hold? I watched you arrive back in Ottemelle Lane. You didn't have much time to write a message or confide in that fat lump of lard who follows you everywhere! Anyway,' the figure chuckled, 'you'll soon be dead by your own hand, and it will be easy enough to depict you as the killer.'

Kathryn shrugged. 'But I know the truth, assassin. So, why not take off that mask? Your face must sweat and itch beneath it. Come on,' she urged. 'I've played the game. We both know I speak the truth.'

One hand came up and the figure pulled back the cowl and peeled back the leather mask and Newington's face, a ghastly colour in candle-light, shone bleakly at her.

'You are a very clever girl, Kathryn,' he hissed, 'far cleverer than I thought.' Newington brought up the crossbow, and from a pouch on his belt placed a second bolt in the groove. He stepped back. 'Do you know,' he continued quietly, 'when that tired old hag the Archbishop and his pompous little clerk Luberon decided to intervene in my games, they looked at the roll of electors for a physician who could help them. That stupid Irishman also.' Newington smiled. 'Of course, I was only too willing to help. The sweating sickness had swept away quite a few physicians. Not enough in my view, but then I came across your name along with your father's.' He shrugged. 'It was just a case of nudging the rest into the trap.' Newington wagged a gloved finger at Kathryn. 'But you were very clever.' Newington spoke like some aggrieved schoolmaster admonishing a pupil. 'Now, come on, Kathryn, there's time enough. Tell me what you do know. I am sure it won't take very long.'

'If I told you what we both know,' Kathryn quipped, 'it won't take us any longer! You're mad, evil and a murderer, Master Newington. You took advantage of the chaos in the city to carry out your revenge against a shrine by murdering pilgrims, innocent men whose only crime was to visit the tomb of Saint Thomas à Becket and belong to a profession which fitted your plans.' Kathryn paused and drew her breath. 'You were well-suited for it, weren't you? You know the city like the back of your hand. A burgess, a man of some importance. You had two other advantages. Your son-in-law is a physician and he had two children whom you always visited. It was so easy, every now and again to collect the key to the herbarium and help yourself to whatever poisons you needed. Who would find out? And if anyone might notice something amiss, that belladonna or foxglove has gone missing, then why not mix in a little flour to conceal the discrepancy? Such powders are ground white. Flour would not hinder their effectiveness and would make it look as if the jars had not been tampered with.' Kathryn forced a smile. 'I was intrigued by that. Why Straunge would find traces of flour on the herbarium floor.'

Newington nodded, gazing expectantly at Kathryn, as if encouraging her on. 'Very good,' he murmured, 'very good indeed. But, as Chaucer's Man of Law says, "Your friends are away in your great need." '

'Then, of course, there are the disguises,' Kathryn continued. 'You are a member of the Guild of Jesus Mass. Every year they put a play on at Saint Holy Cross Church. It would be ever so easy to take a smock and a pair of hose and hide them beneath your alderman's cloak, perhaps use a little paint on your face? Who would notice? People expect to see the obvious. They would never dream that the dirty, grease-stained servitor in a taproom was really a notable alderman. And, of course, you made sure you always moved amongst pilgrims, strangers to the city, who wouldn't recognise you. Matters were helped by the chaos caused by the recent civil war. Your friends and colleagues on the city council are too busy looking after their own affairs and the city is in turmoil. A marvellous cloak for your pastime of slaying innocent men. So easy,' Kathryn concluded. 'You go into a taproom, join a group of pilgrims, commit your foul act and disappear up some alley-way.'

'Enough!' Newington interrupted.

'Oh, come, Master Alderman.' Kathryn edged a little closer. 'Aren't you going to ask me why or how? You know you are mad,' she continued. 'Mad as a March hare.'

Newington's face broke into a snarl. 'And you are a dead bitch!' he grated. He brought the crossbow up. 'But not with an arrow, something more subtle. More fitting to your calling.'

Kathryn licked her lips and breathed in deeply. She could feel her legs tremble and resisted the urge to cry or beg for pity.

'You were very clever,' she continued quietly. 'John Newington, alderman of Canterbury, but you were born the illegitimate son of Christina Oldstrom in Westgate Ward, a seamstress of good family. She raised you, and as soon as you were old enough, you were packed off to London as an apprentice. I suspect that if we searched the records of every church in Canterbury, we would find no trace of the birth of John Newington.' She smiled at the alderman. 'Your mother's name began with "Old," you changed yours to begin with "New," a fine touch. A sign of the times, an indication that you drew a line between what you are now and what you were born. How many years did you spend in London? Ten, twenty? Enough to hide your past. Nevertheless, you felt guilty. You revisited Westgate and saw the poverty in which your mother lived. I suspect you made the bequest to Saint Peter's Church to ease your guilt and hire the doctors who worked in the area. You secretly visited your mother, took care of her every wish. But then she fell ill.'

Newington had his head cocked slightly to one side. He looked pleased, as if Kathryn were faithfully repeating something by rote.

'Yes, yes, you are right, Mistress Swinbrooke. I couldn't publicly recognise my mother, but I did what I could. Then she fell ill. Some hidden wound. I spent good money on this doctor or that. I even paid for a physician from London, but nothing worked. My mother grew thin, she insisted on visiting the shrine, that mauseoleum of dirty bones and relics. I used to don a pilgrim's cloak and meet her at the cathedral. She had such faith, Kathryn! She climbed those steps on her hands and knees and begged for relief.'

Newington's eyes brimmed with tears. Kathryn felt a pang of compassion at how the resentments, humiliation and disappointment had curdled, tipping this man's mind into an evil madness. Newington shrugged like a naughty boy.

'She just wasted away and died.' His voice became thick with emotion. 'Oh, at first, I blamed myself and the doctors, but she died gasping Becket's name with her last breath. Afterwards I would go to the cathedral and watch the pilgrims pour in, spending their hard-earned pennies, and I plotted my revenge.' His face suddenly hardened as Kathryn stepped forward. 'No further, Mistress. You see, I had read Chaucer in London. I bought a copy of his work which, of course, I have since destroyed, but I knew the lines by heart. So I thought I would strike. For every pilgrim mentioned in those tales a person would die in Canterbury. A nice little touch, eh?' Newington tapped his chin. 'I loved those tales. Have you noticed how often potions and poisons appear in them? The revellers in "The Pardoner's Tale," the knight in "The Wife of Bath's Tale"?' He smiled dreamily to himself. 'I used to meet my mother at the great doors of the cathedral. I was always disguised, and I was fascinated by the way no one ever recognised me. Of course, that idiot Faunte kept the council busy.' Newington's face became grave. 'Who cares which princely arse sits on the throne in London?' He looked quickly at the table where the three cups stood. Kathryn remained motionless, hoping Newington would talk until help arrived. The assassin looked quickly at her. 'We really can't wait much longer,' he murmured, as if reading her thoughts. 'Time flies! Time flies! But you mentioned the flour,' he said.

'Yes. Straunge found that on the floor of the herbarium. It was also at the bottom of the jug of wine you gave to Peg the whore.'

'Ah, Mustard Peg. A foul-mouthed bitch! I thought she and that summoner would suit each other. I hired her, told her to meet me at the postern gate, gave her the jug of wine and let her through before hurrying home to my son-in-law's banquet.'

'Your daughter,' Kathryn hastily intervened. 'You have no feelings for her?'

'You know the saying, Mistress Kathryn: "God gives us our family, thank God we can choose our friends!" She's arrogant and haughty. I opposed her marriage to Darryl, though I later relented. The profession provided a fresh source for investment, and in due time, a ready supply of poisons.' Newington grinned. 'How doctors love to talk about this potion or that. And then there's Chaddedon's library.' Newington wagged a finger at Kathryn. 'There isn't much I don't know about poisons.' His face became grave. 'But my grandchildren, I love them. Isn't it ironic'—he tapped the crossbow against his hand—'that you found out through them? You went back to that house this morning and asked who told them the story about

Arcite and Palamon, the two heroes from Chaucer's "Knight's Tale." ' Newington shook his head. 'You shouldn't have done that, using mere babes to trap their grandfather!'

'At first I thought it might be Darryl,' Kathryn replied. 'But the children told me it was you, their grandfather, who loved to tell them stories from Chaucer.'

'You used sweetmeats,' Newington retorted. 'You bribed my grandchildren!'

'Oh, for God's sake!' Kathryn snapped. 'Sooner or later every murderer is trapped. Your grandchildren told me. I remembered how your son-in-law had said he knew nothing about Chaucer, and you claimed the same.'

Kathryn took a fleeting look at the floor-boards behind the alderman and noticed the gaps and cracks there. 'It wasn't just Arcite and Palamon, there were other strands, pieces of information: your membership in the Jesus Mass Guild; you live alone, with no one to watch you. You know Canterbury, possess a key to the postern gate and have access to a ready supply of poisons. But,' Kathryn concluded, 'yes, those innocents trapped you.'

'But they told me,' Newington answered angrily, as if he was more annoyed that his grandchildren had talked to a mere stranger than anything else. 'They told me about your questions, so it was heigh-ho to the cathedral with another proclamation whilst I bribed a soldier to take the message to Ottemelle Lane.' Newington mopped the sweat off his brow with the hem of his robe, though Kathryn noticed he kept the crossbow primed and ready.

'That stupid Irishman's out of the city. Luberon clucks like a chicken. I just knew you would come. You like Murtagh, don't you?'

'What is that to you? And if I hadn't come?'

Newington pulled a face. 'There would be other times, other places, but now you are here! Sweetmeats for my grandchildren!' he snarled. 'Well, I have poisons for you.' Newington pointed to the three cups on the table. 'One contains belladonna, one foxglove, but the other is free of poisons. It's like the game they play in Cheapside in London. Which cup is the lucky one?' Newington raised the crossbow. 'Mistress Swinbrooke, I suggest you try all three.'

'People will suspect,' Kathryn began, trying to control her breathing and calm the panic which threatened to overwhelm her.

'Who will give a damn?' Newington interrupted. He cocked his head sideways. 'Perhaps I'll say you killed yourself? Or were you just another of Sir Thopas's victims?'

'Thopas?' Kathryn exclaimed.

'Yes, yes, you know—the name Chaucer gives himself in the *Canterbury Tales.* I call myself that, the poet of this murderous drama.' Newington shrugged. 'Or perhaps I'll say you were the killer, leave some scrawled message beside you, go quiet for a year and then begin again. Now, now,' Newington urged her with his free hand. 'What's the saying? "Medice sane teipsum, Doctor heal thyself?" Ah, well, in this case it's rather different.' The crossbow was pushed forward. 'Mistress Swinbrooke, please drink. After all, as Chaucer's Wife of Bath says, "I have got of you the mastery".'

Kathryn measured the distance between herself and Newington. It was too far, though she kept her eyes on the floor-boards behind the killer.

'Swinbrooke, drink. Who knows? First time you might be lucky!'

Kathryn moved across to the table and picked up the middle cup, which felt cold and heavy in her hand. She raised it to her lips, smelt the strong claret, then pulled it away.

'I can't!' she said. 'And if you shoot . . .'

Newington smiled faintly. 'Then you're another casualty of war. Perhaps the Irishman will be blamed, or one of his rough soldiers. I'll leave this God-forsaken place as

I entered it, by some back route. There's more holes in the fences and walls of Kingsmead than in a fishing-net.'

Kathryn watched the crossbow intently. Newington, no soldier, was holding it wrongly. He would have to move his hands to release the bolt. She took a step forward.

'I won't drink!'

Newington shifted his grasp, and as he did so, Kathryn hurled the heavy cup towards him, throwing herself sideways against the wall. The crossbow bolt whirled aimlessly past her. Newington fell back, trying to avoid the cup and scrabbling for another crossbow bolt. His heavy riding-boots smashed against the rotten mildewed planks. Kathryn was about to follow when one of the floorboards suddenly snapped, breaking away in a puff of dust. Newington desperately tried to maintain his poise but, as he searched for a foothold, the rest of the weakened floor groaned and snapped, and Newington crashed through, falling to the granite-hard floor below.

Kathryn threw open the door and hurried down the stone steps. In the room below, Newington sprawled in a tumbled heap, one leg twisted awkwardly. At first Kathryn thought he was dead, but then Newington groaned. Kathryn crouched and felt the pulse strong in the man's neck. She stared around, recoiling in disgust at the headless torso of the dog Newington had slaughtered, then tossed into the far corner. Kathryn began to tremble, her legs shook so violently she had to crouch, gasping for breath.

'Calm yourself!' she whispered. 'For God's sake, Kathryn, calm yourself!'

She leaned over, moving the unconscious alderman, but there was no sign of his crossbow. Kathryn took his long stabbing dagger out of his sheath and gripped it tightly.

'Mistress, what is it?'

Kathryn turned. The urchin, the young guard at the gate, stood wide-eyed in the doorway.

Kathryn gestured at him. 'Come here!'

The lad stepped into the room. He glimpsed the mutilated corpse of the dog and turned to retch. He then edged closer, looking fearfully at the prostrate Newington.

'Who be it?' he murmured.

'An evil, sad man,' Kathryn replied.

'Is he dead?'

'No, but he may well wish he was!'

'I didn't see him come.' The boy crossed his stick-like arms, hugging his chest. 'I didn't see him. He must have come by the back route, though I did hear the dog yelp.'

Kathryn forced a smile. 'Come closer!'

The large eyes in the thin whey face stared fearfully back.

'Why?' he asked.

'Because I'm frightened too,' Kathryn confessed. 'I want to hold you!'

The boy trotted round Newington's body and Kathryn clutched him in her arms, pressing his bony body against her. The boy looked down at the knife.

'Is that his?'

'Yes.'

'Can I have it?'

Kathryn smiled and felt a pang of compassion at the boy's thinness. 'What you need, lad,' she replied, 'is a good meal. Tell me about yourself.'

Newington moaned and stirred. Kathryn edged away, taking the boy with her. She wanted to run but she felt too cold, too weak, and she did not want to let Newington slip away.

'Tell me about yourself, boy,' Kathryn repeated.

The lad began to chatter and Kathryn forced herself to listen as he prattled his sad story: vague memories of a mother, then a life of scavenging like a puppy amongst the rubbish of different camps.

'What's your name?' Kathryn interrupted.

'Wuf!' The lad replied.

Kathryn smiled and felt her own warmth and strength return. She stood up and looked down at him. 'Why Wuf?'

'A soldier gave me that name, though he is dead now. I wouldn't smile, Mistress, so he used to blow into my face. When I laughed he said it was due to a woof of air, so I have been called that ever since. I'm also brave,' he continued and pointed down at Newington. 'I heard the crash and I thought you were in danger. Do you have anything to eat?' he added.

'No, I don't.'

'Did he have? Is there anything upstairs?'

Kathryn remembered the cups. 'You are not to go up there, it's an evil place!'

The boy began to describe his last meal, a slab of poached venison, when Kathryn heard the clatter of hoof-beats on the cobbles and, going to the doorway, saw a party of the most wicked-looking bunch of gallows-birds, led by Colum and Holbech, riding into the yard. In the middle of the group, on a small, docile cob, bounced a red-faced, sweating Thomasina who, when she glimpsed her mistress, threw herself down from the saddle and rushed across the yard.

'Mistress Kathryn, what is it? The Irishman sent no message!' Thomasina glared down at the prostrate Newington. 'So, that bastard's involved!' She glanced at the alderman's black cowl and cloak. Thomasina stared at her mistress. 'Newington was the killer?'

'Is he alive?' Colum asked, coming up behind Thomasina. 'Did he hurt you?' He pushed by, shoving the boy aside, and gripped Kathryn by the shoulder.

Kathryn grasped the little boy's hand. 'Yes,' she answered. 'Yes, Newington is the killer. Yes, he did try to murder me, and yes, he's alive, though unconscious.'

Colum stood over the alderman and gave him a vicious kick in the ribs. Newington groaned and opened his eyes.

'Holbech!' Colum roared. 'Rouse this bastard!'

The mercenary swaggered in, picked up some dirty dry straw, produced a tinder and, before Kathryn could object, threw the burning strands down onto Newington's legs. The alderman moaned and squirmed in pain.

'Stop it!' Kathryn ordered.

Colum snapped his fingers, and Holbech, assisted by other soldiers, put the fire out and dragged Newington to his feet. The alderman looked terrible: one side of his face was bruised and his split lips were caked with blood. He looked vacuously at Kathryn and Colum, then sneered.

'Take him out!' Colum commanded. 'Tie him to a horse, hide his face and take him to the castle!'

They watched the soldiers hustle Newington away.

'He will stand trial for his life,' Colum announced, 'but not here; before King's Bench in London. Then he can face the hangman at the Elms!' He looked back at Kathryn. 'How did you know?'

Kathryn smiled. 'Chaucer told me.'

Colum's eyes narrowed.

'I'll tell you later,' Kathryn added, aware that Thomasina was beginning to flap round her like some clucking mother hen.

'Oh,' Kathryn said, 'Upstairs on the table are wine-cups. I think they are full of poison!'

She moved out of the ruined house, still holding the boy by his hand.

'Where are you taking him?' Thomasina asked.

Kathryn stared down at the small urchin.

'He's coming home with me, Thomasina. He's called Wuf. He's very thin, very small and very hungry.' Kathryn grinned at him. 'He's also very brave!'

Thomasina caught the drift of her mistress's mood and clutched the little boy's hand as if he were her long-lost son. Kathryn walked towards the horses as Thomasina and Wuf began to chatter.

'Mistress Swinbrooke!'

Kathryn turned. Colum stood in the doorway. She noticed how tired and unshaven he looked: a typical soldier in his leather jacket, broad sword-belt and thick woollen hose pushed into his high riding-boots. Every time he moved the spurs clinked.

'What is it, Irishman?'

'This is finished?'

'Yes, so it seems.'

'I can still lodge at your house?'

'Of course!'

'Even though I'll bring my ghosts?'

'We all have ghosts, Colum,' Kathryn replied. 'You have the Hounds of Ulster, and God knows the whereabouts of Alexander Wyville!'

Colum, his thumbs looped over his sword-belt, swaggered closer. 'Why did you come here?'

Kathryn shrugged. 'I thought you were in danger.'

The Irishman's eyes softened. 'You came because of me? No woman has ever done that, Mistress Swinbrooke.'

Kathryn turned her back on him and walked a little farther away.

'No woman has ever done that for me!' Colum shouted.

'Well, Irishman,' Kathryn called back over her shoulder, 'then perhaps it's time one of us did!' She turned and grinned. 'After all, as the Wife of Bath says, "A woman's care is God's own gift".'